Grant Allen

The Incidental bishop

Grant Allen

The Incidental bishop

ISBN/EAN: 9783743373181

Manufactured in Europe, USA, Canada, Australia, Japa

Cover: Foto ©Andreas Hilbeck / pixelio.de

Manufactured and distributed by brebook publishing software (www.brebook.com)

Grant Allen

The Incidental bishop

THE INCIDENTAL BISHOP

A NOVEL

BY

GRANT ALLEN

NEW YORK
D. APPLETON AND COMPANY
1898

CONTENTS

PART I.
AUSTRALASIA.

PART II.
ENGLAND.

THE INCIDENTAL BISHOP.

CHAPTER I.

AMONG THE ISLANDS.

"Hard a-starboard!"

The John Wesley turned her slow length; and the two tall cocoa-nut palms on the distant hilltop, which served as seamarks to ships engaged in what was euphemistically called "the Labour Traffic," having been brought into line, she proceeded to steam at a cautious rate into the harbour of Temuka. Its reefs have wrecked many better vessels.

And what a beautifully-chosen name for its purpose, the John Wesley! It smacked of peace and the London Missionary Society. If any meddlesome gunboat of Her Britannic Majesty's fleet, engaged in superintending or suppressing the Labour Traffic aforesaid, had chanced to encounter that long slim steamer, on the prowl after "apprentices," surely the mere sight of the words " John Wesley," legibly carved in gilt letters on her stern, must have disarmed at the first blush the most officious and suspicious of naval officers. The John Wesley, look you! so well-meaning! so innocent! doubtless a vessel engaged in distributing Sunday-School books, and tracts, and cotton pocket-handkerchiefs to the mild but unfortunately heathen inhabitants of those isles of summer. Who could suspect a ship with such a name as the John Wesley of anything blacker than ecclesiastical nonconformity?

That was Tom Pringle's idea when he first signed articles for his memorable voyage. The skipper had assured him (with just a faint quiver of the left eyelid, it is true) that the expedition was wholly concerned with the purchase of *bêche-de-mer*, for export to China, and the peaceful collection of dried cocoa-nut or copra from the Melanesian islands.

Nevertheless, it struck Tom as odd that all hands were on deck when they approached the coast, and that even the sleepy Malay cook with the fat red eyes had an air of alertness and a revolver in his hand, as the shore drew near; it looked as if they were prepared for something more exciting than the peaceable exchange of tobacco and hollands (known locally as " square gin ") for sea-slugs and dried fibres. He began to suspect the meaning of the two dozen sniders on the rack in the cabin, and the handcuffs hung up by the Captain's locker.

Those were the good old days of the early Queensland Labour Traffic. And one may as well admit, without making further ado about it, that the microscopic distinction between the Labour Traffic and the Slave Trade, as they existed thirty years ago, would have puzzled the brains of the minutest casuist. The Traffic, to say the truth, was usually conducted by the primitive method of descending upon an island, buying sturdy young blackfellows, if you could, from their affectionate relations, and stealing them if you could not, by force and arms, without pretence of purchase. Either proceeding was of course just equally illegal; but once get your cargo of human live-stock safe landed in Queensland, and either was winked at by the indulgent labour-employing planter magistrates. To ask no questions, and to take " indentured " servants on the importer's warranty, were the ethics of the times; the John Wesley perhaps was no better and no worse than most other ships then engaged in the Traffic.

Tom Pringle, however, knew nothing of all this; as indeed, how could he? A simple-natured, gently-bred Canadian young man, who had run away to sea as a lad of sixteen from a home in the interior, and spent the last eight years before the mast, he took it for granted that all other sailors were as indifferent honest as himself; and he accepted a berth on a Labour Traffic steamer as readily as he would have accepted it on a Canadian four-master in the grain trade on lake Ontario. He was not specially good, but he was not wholly bad: he was just the average well-educated, adventurous youth who goes to sea or to an Africa diamond-mine, in search of sensation.

The night before, lolling in the forecastle on a balmy star-lit tropical evening, he had observed to the mate, a most accomplished ruffian of the name of Hemmings: "Do you have much trouble in getting the blackfellows to sign their indentures?"

Hemmings stared at him contemptuously for a moment, and sucked in a copious draught of the tobacco-smoke of contemplation. Then he blew it out through his nose in a long slow stream, and waited to consider. Should he enlighten this green-horn now, or let events enlighten him? After all, there's no teacher on earth to equal experience. The mate was a New England blackguard of the first water, trained to humanity on a Louisiana estate, before the war.

He watched the last white curl of smoke disappear in the luminous southern starlight before he answered with the usual seafaring embellishments: "Well, I can't say the niggers give us much trouble, anyhow. They're fond of civilisation. Stands to reason they should be. Just see what it has done for 'em! It's brought 'em big ships, and cloth, and beads, and square gin, and Winchester breech-loaders, and tobacco, and measles, and missionaries, and small-pox, and rum, and the Labour Traffic. Why, a few years ago, say, what outlet was there for an enterprising young native on Temuka, I'd like to know? If he was a chief, well and good; as the sailor said to the Port Admiral: ' You've got a blooming fine berth, old chap; mind you stick to it.' But if he warn't a chief, he couldn't do anything; every durned thing he ever wanted to do was safe as houses to be taboo, and he couldn't even try it. He had jest to lie on his back in the sun and grow fat; and as soon as he was fat enough, by George, if the chiefs didn't use to eat him."

"And now?" Tom asked, looking up.

The mate eyed him again in the mellow starlight with a curious glance of dubious enquiry. He *was* a green 'un, and no mistake; appeared to the mate they'd made a little error in bringing such a raw chap on a job like this one. He took another long pull at his pipe, and blew another curl of most meditative smoke up into the calm, soft tropical air. "Well, naow," he answered slowly, weighing his words as he went, " an in-telligent young native—and some of 'em is almost as intelligent as a dog, I kin tell you —an intelligent young native, with a spark of enterprise in him, . . . kin take advantage of the opportunities afforded him by the Labour Traffic. He kin sign his indentures—" the mate glanced sideways again at his unconscious hearer; "—or rather, not knowing how to write, he kin put his cross agin his name on a paper; and then he kin be taken over sea to Queensland, free of charge, in a commodious steamer; while our own flesh and blood, if *they* want to emigrate, have to pay their passage in the steerage quarter of a beastly emigrant vessel. Then he kin work seven years, all found, on an estate in Queensland, where the Queen's government gives him medical attendance, and everything else thrown in, gratis. And he kin get converted; he kin find religion; he kin have the blessings of Christianity conferred upon him for nothing, with as much square gin as he wants, into the bargain. And at the end of his time,—well, he kin return to his own home, with a felt hat, an' a pair of pants, an' a breech-loader rifle, and be as good as a chief himself, and shoot other blackfellows, and cook 'em, and eat 'em. Oh, there ain't any denying it, no flies on the Labour Traffic: it's been a durned fine thing for the march of intellect in the South Sea Islands; it's brought home to their own doors the blessings of civilisation." The mate took another pull, as he spoke, at the particular blessing which was nearest, save one, to his own heart; the solitary exception being of course hollands.

"Do they ever give any trouble?" Tom enquired again, musing. "—Want to fight and so forth?"

Hemmings laughed outright. "Oh, you *are* an innocent one!" he cried. "Why, mister, you don't suppose savages lift their hats politely when they meet you on the beach, and say, 'Mr. Hemmings, I reckon? Step in and have a drink, sir.' Blackfellows is blackfellows; and there ain't no counting on 'em. They're always a bit suspicious of the man that tries to civilise 'em. Didn't they kill Captain Cook? and wasn't it Captain Cook that first introduced the blessings of civilisation to the Pacific islands, when the natives in their blindness knew no better nor to bow down to stocks and stones, instead of buying bottled beer, and couldn't so much as tell you the right word for tobacco? Didn't they kill Bishop Patteson—and sarve him right, too; what in thunder did he want to come interfering for in a sphere as is better left to the pioneers of civilisation in the square gin and labour trades? *They're* the people for the South Seas; you bet your bottom dollar on it. They understand the natives, and they understand the trade, and they ain't hampered by any of your all-fired Exeter Hall nonsense. A man *must* make money." And the mate brought down his fist on his own lean knee with a fervour of conviction which there was no gainsaying.

"Then we may have a brush with them?" Tom enquired. He was an average young Briton, neither better nor worse than most others of his age, though superior to the run of sailors in education; and to say the truth, he would not wholly have minded the chance of a fight, provided he believed the natives to be the aggressors.

Hemmings stroked his goatee beard. *This* was more like the right spirit! "Don't you be afeard, young man," he answered, staring hard at him. "If it's a brush you want, you stand as fair a chance of seeing some fun with the blackfellows aboard the John Wesley as aboard any other vessel engaged in the Traffic on the South Pacific. Captain Ford ain't the build of man to stand their nonsense. Every blackfellow has got to mind his p's and q's when Captain Ford's about. A nigger in these latitudes ain't got any p's, no doubt, and don't know any q's, being just a poor benighted heathen, ignorant of his alphabet; but he's bound to acquire 'em where Captain Ford's around, I kin tell you; for Captain Ford takes care a blackfellow shall mind 'em, whether he's got 'em or not; and mind 'em he must, or Captain Ford will ask the reason why, with the muzzle of a Winchester."

Tom laughed unconcernedly. He did not realise the full import of the mate's remarks; and if they only meant that aggressive natives would be kept at arm's length, why, Tom rather looked forward than otherwise to the fun of a skirmish. He turned into his berth that night, when his watch was over, without much compunction; but he fell asleep, repeating to himself a stray line of Horace, which he had learnt when he was a boy at the Grammar School in Canada; for he was not without the rudiments of a polite education. He hadn't thought of Horace for six years or so, he fancied; but the mate had said: " A man *must* make money "; which brought him back by a curious side-touch to a forgotten hexameter —something about " Rem facias, rem: si possis, recte; si non, quocunque modo, rem."

CHAPTER II.

A BRUSH WITH THE NATIVES.

THIS morning, however, Tom was clearly aware that something unusual was now expected. Every one was on deck, and every one's face wore an eager look of keen expectation.

They were steaming cautiously round a headland into a dark open harbour. Black basalt crags hemmed it in. Tom took it for the crater of an extinct volcano. In shape it was absolutely circular, with tall walls of cliff, broken only by a single narrow and shallow opening, which he judged at sight to be the lip through which lava had flowed in prehistoric eruptions. Just opposite this lip, three conical hills rose abruptly in the foreground, backed up by the great rampart of sheer basalt precipice. Tom was no geologist, but he could see at a glance that this rampart represented the old funnel of the crater, while the three small hills were clearly cones of erupted ash and pumice-stone. A merciless tropical sun beat hard on black cliff and white hillock. The whole was thickly covered, however, by a beautiful mantle of tropical greenery; cocoa-nut palms waved on the slopes of the three hills, and bamboos sprang feathery from the black clefts of the precipice. In and out among the bush that draped the lesser hills rose groups of native huts, surrounded by flaming crimson hibiscus bushes. It was one of the most glorious harbours Tom had ever beheld; and its beauty was increased by the numberless small waterfalls which tumbled in sheets of white foam from the precipice above down the ravines to the foreshore. They suggested delicious pictures of romantic bathing-places—deep basins shaded by thick forest foliage, where one could spend the whole day in swimming and diving.

Tom was the only person on deck, however, who paid the slightest attention to this exquisite scene. The others were all standing in very attentive attitudes, engaged in watching the hurry and bustle that possessed the native town, at the sudden appearance of a European steamer.

Tom looked round also, and saw at once that the arrival of these pioneers of civilisation had unaccountably thrown the Melanesian population into a fervour of panic. Before the John Wesley had rounded the point, almost (among rocks and reefs most perilous to seamen), he

could see hasty preparations going on in the
wattled villages that crowned the three hillocks.
Mothers caught up their naked black children in
their arms, and fled shrieking to the paths that
wound in zigzag up the precipice. Young girls
rushed after them with every sign of terror. Men
emerged from the huts with long spears in their
hands, and advanced towards the shore, threateningly, brandishing their weapons as they went,
and crying aloud with fierce and angry gestures.
The whole district looked at once like an ant-
hill stirred up by the foot; the black human ants
were removing their young, or saving their own
skins, or showing fight against the intruder, in
a way that absurdly recalled their insect proto-
types. And a blazing hot sun revealed it all with
tropical distinctness.

As Tom stood and gazed, immensely interested in this strange sight—for it was his first
voyage to the South Pacific—a voice at his side
suddenly roused him from his inaction. It was
Hemmings who spoke. " Here, you, Pringle,"
he cried, catching Tom by the arm, " what are
you standing staring there for? This is business,
young man! Just you catch that revolver!"

He handed it as he spoke, with a cutlass into
the bargain. Tom took them, half bewildered.
He began to be aware with a sudden start of

surprise that the " little brush " was at hand in real earnest.

"And mind you," Hemmings went on ; " none of your durned Puritanical nonsense here! You've shipped on a Labour Vessel, and you've got to accommodate yourself. We don't want no passengers, and we don't want no neutrals. It's fight, or get speared; either the niggers will do it, or a civilised six-shooter."

Tom hurried to the gunwale, and looked across towards the shore, whence canoes were shoving off through the surf as fast as the ex-cited natives could man them.

Captain Ford stood close by, with a very resolute air,—a large, loose man, with a Napo-leonic nose, inflamed by drinking. He was not quite such a ruffian, to look at, as the mate; but he was a determined person, and his business was slave-making. On occasions like this, he kept studiously sober. Glancing at the foremost canoes, he held his hand up for a sign. Tom guessed at once it meant " Is it peace or war? " for even the skipper preferred buying coolies to fighting for them. But the men of Temuka knew the John Wesley and its ways too well. A shout of defiance and a fierce clatter of spears was the instant answer.

" Show them the square gin," the skipper

said, very calmly. He was a phlegmatic scoundrel.

A sailor held up three of the coveted bottles, while another displayed an empty case with inviting gestures. The mate himself flung out a few packages of tobacco. But the natives proceeded to shout threateningly as before; meanwhile, the women and children kept flying to the hills, while all in the villages was bustle of preparation.

" Fair trade's no go," the skipper said, turning to Hemmings. " It's no use trying them with square gin this journey. They remember old Noumau. Give 'em a shot, Hemmings; give 'em a shot. That'll bring 'em to reason! "

In a second, a loud boom resounded from the big gun, and a shot ploughed its way through the canoes, dashing foam right and left, and upsetting one of them. There was a scramble for life. The natives swam and struggled in the water like tadpoles. It was clear some of them were wounded. The skipper paused a moment to judge the effect of this practical warning.

For a minute or two, the blackfellows shouted and chattered incoherently. Then a retreat was beat. The canoes began to put back, the men still brandishing their spears in anger. " We can't do anything just yet," the skipper said, turning to his second in command. " No business here this morning. They won't come near now, and we can't land in face of them; if we wait till night, they'll have made up their differences with the nearest villages, and they'll all swarm out in their canoes to surround us. Hemmings, we must steam out again and land a party to take them at their dances from the shore in the rear. Then we can fire a shot or two to divert the main body, and keep the rest engaged till you've crept round to surprise them."

The John Wesley steamed out again, obedient to the bell, in her slow majestic fashion. Tom could see the natives had very rudimentary notions of strategy; for the moment she turned, they seemed to consider the game was up, and put off again in their canoes, deriding and insulting her. It was evident they thought their mere show of opposition had frightened away the well-armed white men. Captain Ford smiled grimly at this childish demonstration, for he knew they would find out their mistake before long. He took action calmly. The John Wesley steamed off some four miles to northward, past a region of mangrove swamps, to a hard surf-beaten beach where landing was possible. Then the boats were put out, and most hands ordered into them. Tom went with the rest, a little doubtful now as to the legality of this method of recruiting apprentices, but too full of the excitement and novelty of the occasion to find much room just then for mere moral compunctions.

They rowed through the sobbing breakers of a great white reef towards a shelving hard, and landed, unseen, in a bay by the shore a few miles from the harbour. A native or two rushed out from a group of huts close by; but a well-directed shot or so drove them into the bush once more. There, they skulked behind the trees, and fired, for they were armed with old patterns of discarded rifles; but it was impossible to see them. "Single file!" the skipper called out in a military voice; and the men, forming in single file, followed him along a track that led tortuously through the forest. The skipper walked first; it was a tangled path, along which two men could not go abreast. Tom had never had a harder march in his life, for the gnarled roots and twisted stems of the creepers were troublesome, and the ground was boggy; besides which, every now and again, with a sudden clash, the natives beat tom-toms, and yelled, and peppered them from behind a tree, disappearing as instantly. The jungle was close and damp: the air steamed: it was the climate of an orchid house. Still, the skipper marched on, as along a road that he knew; while the natives fell behind, not caring for the rest, as soon as they saw their own little group of huts in the ravine by the bay was not seriously menaced. Even then, the mosquitoes made each step an annoyance, while leeches dropped from the trees as they passed beneath them.

The whites continued through the wood for a mile or two in silence. Not a word was spoken. Suddenly, a turn in the tortuous path led them again to the shore. There, a glade opened up, and to Tom's great surprise, they burst upon a body of young people dancing. It was a strange, weird scene. The whole party halted and drew itself up in line for a moment. The dancers, too much occupied in their dance to be conscious of anything else, never even observed the arrival of the white men. In a second the skipper saw he had reached his aim in the nick of time: this was a great annual religious ceremony. Dozens of young men and women, with their smooth black limbs half draped in garlands, were moving up and down in a measured rhythm, with painted faces. "It's a *meké*," the skipper said low; " stand aside, boys, and take care; I thought this would be on: we can catch the whole lot of them."

The young men and women swayed voluptuously backward and forward in the shade of the trees, their shining black bodies silhouetted against the foam on the shore. They moved like the figures on a Celtic cross, in strange rhythmic curves and intertwining circles. Clearly, they had heard nothing of the arrival of the steamer at Temuka harbour: their tom-toms must have drowned even the noise of the cannon. Besides, in their ecstasy of religious abandonment, all outer events were wholly forgotten. Tom could see their festival was the Eleusinian mystery of some South Sea Ashtaroth. It was at once a dance, a prayer, a hymn, a procession. Men and women chanted slow their mystic chorus in line, keeping time to the tom-toms. Louder and louder grew the strains: quicker and quicker became the motions of their bodies. " Hold back till I give the word," the skipper muttered in a low voice; " then, the moment I say, *Go*, rush forward and seize them! "

At the time, it struck Tom this was the merest slave-raid. But though it revolted his sense of right to take part in such an attack, he had not depth of moral conviction enough to make him hold back from joining in it. He awaited the signal breathlessly. " Now, *go!* " the skipper cried; and almost before Tom could realise what was happening, the sailors had rushed forward, like a body of wild beasts, and were securing the likeliest young men and women with cords and handcuffs.

The whole thing took but a moment. At once, the shore was alive with tumult. The natives were numerous, but unarmed; for though they used spears in their dance, the points were blunted; they were like ornamental fencing foils. A few of the medicine men or sorcerers behind, beating tom-toms and directing the dance, had long knives, to be sure; but these were of little use against the white man's fire-arms. Captain Ford stood close by, with his revolver raised; four sailors, beside him, pointed rifles at the natives. The men were cowed; the women, screaming and terrified, rushed wildly towards the bush, and were allowed for the most part to escape, for the planters only require girls in the proportion of one to every four " apprentices." In an incredibly short time, some forty or fifty young men had been secured and handcuffed; they grovelled now on the ground at the skipper's feet, with the muzzles of the rifles covering them all in turn, and waited to learn what fate was reserved for them.

As Tom, too, waited and wondered, the John Wesley hove in sight, while the boats in which they had landed came paddling slowly round the corner. Then Tom saw the whole attack had been carefully planned and ably executed. The skipper knew of this festival, and had counted upon its occurrence. He had created a diversion at Temuka harbour, to take off the attention of the main body of blackfellows, and then had surprised the unarmed young men and women where their capture was easiest.

The empty boats rowed landward. One by one, the captured natives were marched to the shore and huddled into them carelessly, tied hand and foot,—bundled into the boats much as one has seen fowls packed in crates for railway travelling. They resisted very little, for they saw all was up: but those who did resist were quietly knocked on the head with the butt-end of a rifle, and, half-stunned by the blow, forced hastily into the gig. Then, a strong net was fastened across them, beneath the thwarts, as one has seen it fastened over a calf in a market cart. Altogether, not the slightest recognition was given to the fact that a Melanesian, after all, is a vertebrate animal. Tom began to perceive the true inwardness of that extremely elastic phrase, the Labour Traffic, and to understand that he had been inveigled into a man-stealing expedition.

As they busied themselves about putting off,

the natives behind, now recovering from their panic, began to show their heads once more among the bush in the background, or even to advance towards the shore, with sticks and stones and other improvised weapons. The skipper's cue was not to hesitate. "Fire!" he said shortly to the four men with rifles; and at the word, four bullets whizzed in among the blackfellows. Two of them fell wounded; the rest, not waiting to help them or to see whether they were dead, rushed back pell-mell under cover of the jungle.

"Now, row off," the skipper said. "To the ship at once! We've got as much stock as we shall get at Temuka."

CHAPTER III.

RIVAL PIONEERS OF CIVILISATION.

Tom took his place at the oars, feeling decidedly uncomfortable. It was an ugly business. For all he knew, those two blackfellows might be dead, and he himself might have been accessory to their murder. In any case, he had been inveigled, however little on his own account by malice aforethought, into a slave-making raid on a Pacific island. To increase his discomfort, the skipper gazed across at him with a sardonic smile. "*Bêche-de-mer* and copra, you see!" he said calmly. "And in a ship like this! Oh, my soul, Tom Pringle, you *are* a fresh one!"

Tom rowed on in silence towards the hateful black hull of the slim John Wesley.

They had passed the reef, where the sea swirled and seethed like a boiling cauldron, and were nearing the ship, when a sudden cry from the skipper made Tom look up in astonishment.

"Why, what's this, Hemmings?" the skipper exclaimed, looking anxiously forward. " Blessed

if that canoe there ain't flying the British colours!"

All hands looked in front. The skipper was
quite right. Four well-manned canoes were
sweeping round the point from Temuka harbour;
and the first of them displayed the Union Jack,
waved prominently in front by a man in a pith
helmet.

The skipper gazed again. Then he whistled
long and hard. "Blamed if it ain't one of them
confounded missionaries!"

Still, the four canoes rowed straight on, head-
ing steadily between the boats and the John
Wesley. "And he means to cut us off," Hemmings put in, acquiescing.

"I shall fire," the skipper said briefly.

"He's a white man," Hemmings answered.
"It's an act of piracy. You're boss on your own
ship, of course; but if I was you, Captain Ford,
I'd be careful."

"White man or no white man, what does he
want to come interfering with the Labour Traffic for?" the skipper answered angrily. "We've
got to have labourers; and we've got to get 'em
the best way we can. If it wasn't for these confounded white-livered missionaries, we wouldn't
have half the trouble. I shall give him a piece
of my mind.—Fire a shot across her bows, Jim."

The man he had ordered fired without a second's hesitation. But the canoe, never heeding the shot, came on till it was within hailing distance.

Then a weather-beaten man, with an open honest face, stood up in her bow and shouted. "Don't shoot," he said quietly. "We come on a mission of peace. We only want to ask what you are doing in our waters."

"What the blank is that to you?" the skipper answered, scowling. "We're trading among the islands. Don't interfere with free trade. Keep your distance, or we'll fire." Then he added lower: "He don't know we've got 'em already. If he comes near enough to see we have stock aboard, he'll make mischief in Sydney."

The man with the open face took no notice of the prohibition. If skippers can be resolute, so too can missionaries; and Tom realised at that moment that it needs a brave man to take his life in his hands and settle down alone among these savage islanders.

He waved his hand to his crew and drew a little nearer; then he called out again: "Are you Bully Ford?"

"My name is Ford," the skipper answered. "If you choose to call me Bully, that's your own affair. It's a name I've been called by. And

I allow I ain't one to stand any blamed non-sense, from blackfellows or from missionaries."

The weather-beaten man gave some order in an unknown tongue to his men. They seemed to have implicit confidence in him, for they went on rowing. The canoe was now quite close, and the missionary stood up in the bows. Then he gave a sudden start. "Why, you've got natives aboard!" he exclaimed, half incredulously.

The skipper made up his mind with the rapid decision of a man of action, engaged in a dangerous trade, and accustomed to face emergencies with instant resolution. He turned to his men. "Fire at them," he said quietly.

Two of the men hesitated. It is one thing to shoot unknown and nameless savages; quite another thing to shoot an English missionary. But the other two had no such scruples. The South Seas in those days were fairly remote; the Queen's writ did not run beyond Fiji. Two rifles snapped sharply; in the canoe, a black man disappeared into the water, and the white man fell back, wounded, into the arms of his followers.

Still, the foremost canoe, in which he lay, moved steadily on. The others followed it at a cautious distance.

The missionary came alongside. He was bleeding profusely. "Bully Ford," he said slowly, " I think you have killed me.   But thank God, you have killed this iniquitous traffic."

The skipper gazed at him with a shade of remorse and horror.   Then his coarse nature reasserted itself.   " Row back," he cried to the men.   " Back at once to the steamer!"

Tom flung down his oar.   " Back?" he cried. " And leave him here?"

" Young fellow," the skipper said, " if you're insubordinate, I shall know how to deal with you."

" Oughtn't never to have shipped him," Hemmings murmured slowly.

But Tom's blood was up now.   " You shall *not* row back," he cried.   " You shall take him aboard and nurse him.   The man's dying; that's clear; but you shall not abandon him.—Look here, you mates," he went on, turning to his fellow-sailors.   " He's a white man, anyhow. Bring him on board, and let him die, and give him Christian burial."

There was a moment's hesitation.   Then Hemmings bent forward.   " Better do as he says," he suggested.   " It'll save trouble afterwards.   Things are getting rough on the islands for the Labour Traffic."

The skipper gave way sullenly.   " Pull him on board!" he answered.

"Three of the sailors took hold of the wounded man. The Temukans, raising a loud cry, seemed as if they would resist. Tom could not understand them, of course, but he guessed fairly enough the general meaning of their wild cries of "Oh, my father, stop with us!" "Do not take him away!" "He is our friend, our father!"

The wounded man raised his hand and said something in Melanesian to his body-guard of converts. The natives gave way at once. With loud wailings, they let him go, and rested on their paddles in impressive silence.

"Anyhow," the skipper said calmly, "we've put a spoke in *his* wheel! He won't try any more to interfere with the Labour Traffic."

Tom laid the wounded man's head on his own lap, and resumed his oar, much incommoded by the struggling and writhing natives on the bottom. "Row on!" the skipper said again; and they rowed on steadily. Ten minutes more brought them up to the John Wesley.

They lifted the wounded man aboard; then they began one by one to transfer the live-stock. As fast as each native was put on board, he was carefully ironed. The women wailed a little with low savage growls, but the men for the most part took the whole affair quietly. They knew well enough for what they were wanted, now, and they resigned themselves to their fate with the stoicism of the savage. After all, it was better than being cooked and eaten, the usual end of their race when captured by enemies of their own people. Some of them even laughed at each other's plight; and all took blows with incredible composure. The sailors knocked them about as drovers knock about sheep. Nobody seemed to regard them as anything more than so much useful and insensitive merchandise.

"Now," the skipper said, when all was taut on board, and the "stock" had been carefully secured on deck, " off to Brisbane at once! The sooner the better, before these devils can get together their war-canoes to attack us."

CHAPTER IV.

Tom had wondered on the journey from Singapore to Temuka why the John Wesley carried so large a crew; she had more hands aboard, he saw, than any steamer of her size, peaceably engaged in local trade of dried cocoa-nut, could be expected to require. But he was unaccustomed to the South Seas and harboured no mean suspicions; indeed, he had never heard of the Labour Traffic before he signed articles at Singapore; nor had he sailed east of Calcutta on any previous voyage. Now, he understood that the crew was not a crew alone; it was also an armed body. Bully Ford needed a compact force of men, both to assist him in securing native lads and women, and to prevent them from rising in case of emergency. The consequence was that Tom's services were not much needed on the return voyage. The skipper saw at once he was little to be trusted on such an errand, and preferred to tell him off as sick-room attendant upon the wounded missionary, rather than let him see too much of what went on on deck with the captured Melanesians. "He's a sniveller at heart," he observed to Hemmings.

The missionary was seriously wounded, in addition to which he had suffered severely for some years past from the climate and its hardships; Tom did not think he could reach Brisbane alive. Neither did the skipper,—which was why he tolerated him. From the skipper's point of view, it was safer business to give out that the missionary had been wounded in an accidental scuffle with the natives; and that to prevent his being killed and eaten by his flock, the John Wesley had taken him off and tended him carefully. Bully Ford could thus turn his act of piracy into one of humanity. The man was sure to die before they hove in sight of Brisbane. As soon as *he* was dead, nothing could be easier than to clap that fellow Pringle into irons as an insubordinate sailor; and who then would believe his unsupported evidence?

The missionary was a young man about Tom's own age—tall, wiry, sunburnt. He had a bushy beard, and a generally unkempt appearance; but beneath it all, Tom could see marks of a generous disposition and a profound enthusiasm. His name was Cecil Glisson. When Tom first heard that name, he could hardly have believed how deeply familiar it was destined to become to him in future.

The missionary's wound was in his right lung; but Glisson took little notice of it. He had known his days were numbered even before he was shot; and his one hope now was that he might manage to live till he reached Brisbane, so as to put an end by his martyrdom to this infamous traffic. Tom told him the plain truth about his presence on the John Wesley: honesty understands honesty; and Glisson believed him. As Tom sat by the wounded man's bedside, preparing arrowroot with Swiss milk, a friendship gradually sprang up between them. "Could you read to me?" Glisson asked wistfully, in an interval of his fever.

Tom hesitated. "Read what? We have nothing to read here."

"Not a Bible?"

"No, nothing at all, except the charts and the South-Sea Sailing Directions."

The dying man hesitated. "I have a Greek Testament," he said; "it's in my pocket there, hanging up. I always carry it about with me. But my eyes are too weak, and of course *you* can't read it."

"I haven't read Greek for some time," Tom

said, hesitating: "and I don't suppose I should understand it. But I think I could just manage to read out the words, if that would be any good. I'll have a try, anyhow."

Glisson opened his weary eyes and looked up at the sailor in surprise. "You, read Greek?" he exclaimed in astonishment. "No, no! You must be mistaken."

Tom felt in the missionary's pocket, and found what he sought—a small and much thumb-marked Testament. He opened it at the place where it naturally bent back, the third of Second Corinthians. Then, in a clear soft voice, he began reading slowly the sonorous Greek, giving the full value to his open Eta's and Omega's.

Glisson listened with dreamy eyes. "How did you learn?" he asked at last slowly.

"I was at a grammar school in Canada," Tom answered. "I learnt a tidy bit of Latin there, and a little Greek. But what surprises me most is this; I never knew much: yet I think I understand the Greek better now, though I haven't looked at it since, than I did when I was a schoolboy."

"That's natural," Glisson replied. "Mere age often does it. You catch at things better now. Can you follow what you read?"

"I think, every word of it."

"You read as if you did. You must read to me often. Go on now. It soothes me."

Tom read on and on, and saw that Glisson was right. Mere age told. He could recollect fairly well the run of the epistle in the English version; and the Greek suggested it to him wherever he forgot it. Besides, he knew he had a natural gift of languages. He had picked up some words of Arabic when he was cruising in the Red Sea; and even on board the John Wesley he was learning already a phrase or two in Melanesian from the talk of the poor creatures tied up in pairs on the deck of the steamer.

Glisson listened with his eyes shut. At last he opened them slowly. "It's like old times," he said. "It reminds me of the days when I was reading for orders."

"You are a clergyman of the Church of England?" Tom asked.

"Yes; ordained in England."

"An Oxford man?"

Glisson gave a little start as of surprise. "Oh, nothing like that," he answered. "A poor waif and stray. I was an orphan in a Liverpool foundling hospital. I had no friends on earth, except good Bishop Patteson. He befriended me as a boy; and when I was growing up, he had me sent to a theological college, where I learnt these things. It was he who had me ordained, and brought me out here to help him."

That made Tom feel more at home at once with his patient. The honest desire not to seem more than he was drew Tom towards him instantly.

From that moment forth, they talked much together; much, that is to say, considering Glisson's condition. The missionary told his sailor friend all about his youth at the orphanage, and his life at the theological college; more still about his work among the savages of Temuka. Most of them, of course, were still heathen and cannibals; but Glisson had collected a little band about him. He loved his blackfellows; and Tom could clearly see that he longed to live till they reached Brisbane, mainly because he thought his own death might redound to the putting down of this infamous slave-trade.

But he grew worse daily, in the stifling heat of his cabin, in spite of all Tom could do for him. His wound was serious. Each time Tom came on deck, the skipper asked with a grim smile: " Well, how's your patient? " And each time, when Tom answered: " Growing worse, I fear," the skipper nodded, well pleased, and muttered the same words: " What do these people want to go interfering with free trade for? "

At last, about three days off from Brisbane, Tom was watching by the wounded man's side, when he saw Glisson suddenly start and lift one hand up. Then a red stream gurgled from mouth and nostrils. Tom knew what had happened. Hæmorrhage of the wounded lung. He was bleeding to death internally. It was all up with him.

He held Glisson in his arms, very white and pallid. The missionary's lips just moved. Tom bent over to listen. " Tell them in England what has happened—let my blood be the last that is shed in this wicked traffic."

He fell back, dead. And Tom knew that Bully Ford was that innocent man's murderer.

CHAPTER V.

BULLY FORD'S LIVE-STOCK.

ON deck, the skipper sat discoursing business with his assistant, Hemmings. "First-rate stock, Hemmings," he ejaculated. He was a judge of slave-flesh.

"Lot of trouble to get 'em, though," the mate responded.

"Ay, these missionaries are ruining the trade," the skipper admitted, pensively. "There ain't no two ways about it. This is as fine-looking, clean, healthy a lot of stock as you'd wish to see: yet he wants to stop us from taking them. Why, when I first began supplying labour to the Brisbane market, we could recruit economically: hands could be sold at a pound a head, easy. No nonsense then about indentures or contracts. We just came down on an island, carried 'em off without a word, and sold 'em, open, to the highest bidder. Now, they've got all this new-fangled rubbish about apprentices. There's no knowing where it'll end. Last time

I was in Sydney, I heard talk of a Government Inspector to sail on every vessel, and the owners to pay him twenty pound a month. It ain't fair to capital. It 'ud be the ruin of the Traffic." (The amenities of literature compel me to suppress the running fire of oaths which agreeably diversified Bully Ford's style, adding point and picturesqueness to his mildest sentence: but I do so with regret, for the skipper's conversation was estimated to contain a larger percentage of coarseness and profanity to the square mile than any other man's on the South Pacific.)

"That's so," the mate assented. "We are a sight too much governed. Same at Brisbane. When we got there, do you mind, we used to march the stock in gangs to the verandah of the store, and leave 'em there for inspection by intending purchasers. Now, what have you got to do? You've got to clothe 'em, and feed 'em, and see they don't resist when folks come to buy them, or the magistrates 'll say they ain't willing immigrants. Willing immigrants, indeed! As if anybody believed it! What I hate in this world is its confounded humbug. If you're doing a trade in slaves, why the thunder can't you say so?"

"You're right there," Ford replied. "If things goes on like this, we shall have to do everywhere like they do in Fiji—take off your hat to the natives and beg 'em to be kind enough to do a day's work for you. How's work to be done, I'd like to know, if you can't get the boys? We shall have to do like they do in Fiji, I say. 'Very good; you go along a Melbourne along a me? Very good ki-ki. Pay very good. Pay money. Plenty shop. You buy what you like. You very good fellow; me very good master.' Cringing to a Kanaka! Yah! I couldn't stoop to it!"

"Nor me," the mate continued. "It makes me sick to hear 'em. 'Master no take you, suppose you no like: me put you ashore at place belong a you.' And then, all that rot about eighteen pounds clear at the end of three yam crops! 'You no be frightened. Captain good fellow man; he no fight; he no swear at you; plenty eat; plenty square gin; plenty Mary belong a Malo; plenty young man belong a your place; all missionary boy; me missionary man.' Is *that* the sort of way for a white man to behave to niggers?"

"Besides, it ain't humane," Bully Ford said, apologetically; for even blackguards make apologies to virtue. "Natives bring a woman down to your boat, tied hand and foot; and they want a stick of tobacco for her. She's got into a row, and they're bound to punish her. But she ain't a willing recruit, and you say: ' Can't take her.' Well, what do them natives do? Just carry her back, and roast her."

As he spoke the words, Tom Pringle's head appeared above the companion.

" What does that sneaking chap want?" the skipper asked.

" He's dead," Tom answered.

" A good job too," the skipper said. " Well, throw him overboard!"

" What, now—without waiting? and without burial?" Tom exclaimed.

The skipper eyed him curiously. " Young man," he said, with philosophic calm, " it strikes me very forcibly you've mistaken your vocation. A labour vessel don't pretend to be a missionary ship."

Tom glanced at the " stock," packed on deck like sardines, in the baking heat, and admitted at once the truth of this reflection.

But before anything more could pass between them, the mate jumped up with a sudden exclamation. " Hullo there," he cried. " Look to starboard, captain!"

Bully Ford looked round and gave a long low whistle.

Tom's eyes followed theirs. Away off on the

horizon, a steamer was in sight, bearing down at full steam in the direction of the John Wesley. The skipper seized his binoculars. Tom's unaided sight did not avail to tell him it was a gun-boat cruiser; but he guessed as much from the skipper's sudden look of dismay and disappointed anger.

"Full steam ahead?" the mate enquired.

The skipper stared again. "No good," he answered, with his usual quick determination; for, bully and scoundrel as he was, he was a born commander. "She steams faster than us. If we run for it, she'll run us down, and the chase will tell against us. We must chuck the stock. That's the only way. If they come here and catch us, it's piracy, I reckon."

Tom hardly yet understood what this prompt determination involved; but whatever it **was,** he saw Bully Ford intended it.

"Bring up that dead devil-dodger first," Ford went on, closing his mouth like a rat-trap.

The mate disappeared. In another minute, he and a sailor came up, carrying Glisson's body, like a dead weight between them.

Nobody spoke a word. One of the sailors fastened to it a heavy leaden shape, of a sort that Tom had noticed in a bunker on the main deck, and had examined with no little wonder as to what might be their purpose.

" Chuck it over to leeward! " Bully Ford said. The gunboat was coming from windward.

Without a word of reply, the sailors carried the body to the lee gunwale, which was also the side remotest from the gunboat, and flung it over heavily. One—two—three, and it disappeared with a slight splash into the angry water. The wake closed over it. For a fair sea was running, and the wind rose steadily.

" Now, below with the stock! " Ford exclaimed, without a shudder.

The sailors proceeded to hurry the men and women to the hold, one by one; Tom hardly knew why; but a minute later, he saw it was to prevent resistance and the chance of a rising. Handcuffed as they were, they might still have given trouble had they known what was coming.

One man alone was left on deck at the last. Meanwhile, the John Wesley continued on her course, as if she had never even noticed the gunboat, though it was signalling now from its distant position.

" Weight! " the skipper said. Quick as lightning, two sailors fastened a weight to the blackfellow's feet. " Now, over! " They lifted him, struggling and screaming, in their arms, carried him to the lee gunwale, and dropped him quietly into the dark sea like a bale of goods, as they had dropped the corpse. With a wild shriek he fell. The shriek was choked by the rushing water. He sank like lead to the bottom. The rollers closed over him. "Good money gone!" was all the skipper's comment.

"Next!" Bully Ford said calmly. The sailors brought up another in turn from the hold, where Tom could see two of their number standing guard with six-shooters over the excited black-fellows. The natives did not know exactly what was happening, indeed, but they suspected mischief, and rushed about wildly or crouched in terror. Quickly and silently, with military order, the sailors brought up one man after another. As each reached the deck, a weight was fastened with mechanical regularity to his feet, he was carried to the edge, and, with a "One, two, three," heaved over into the black water. The monotonous repetition of the loud cries, the sudden shriek, the dull thud upon the surface, the immediate and ghastly silence as the shriek was stifled, sickened Tom as he looked. He had a vague suspicion that *his* turn would come next, when they had finished with the blackfellows.

Time after time the same horrible scene recurred. They worked their way through the

men, and proceeded to the women. These met
their fate with more sullen resignation. Perhaps
they were better accustomed to brutal treatment.
As the last was just reached, a shot across their
bows ploughed up the water. Bully Ford glanced
aside. "Ha, she's angry," he said, "because
we don't notice her signals. But I'd knock this
ship's brains out on a reef, if I could, sooner'n
let her catch us."

He rang the bell to stop her. The engine
reversed. Then he glanced with cold eyes at
Tom. "Go below, sir," he said shortly. "I
ain't got time left to chuck you overboard just
now; but by George, if once we run past this
tight place, I'll break every bone in your sneaking white body. A white man, and you'd want
to side with niggers! He's under arrest, Hemmings. Mind you keep your eye on him."

What happened next, Tom never really knew.
He slunk down the companion, but Hemmings
did not follow him. By a sort of blind instinct,
he took refuge in the empty bunk where Glisson
had lain dying. The missionary's clothes hung
idly on a peg by the door of the cabin. A sudden idea seized Tom. If the gunboat came up
and searched, as likely as not every man on board
would be arrested on a charge of piracy; for
pirates they were, and now he knew it. In that

case, his protestations of innocence would avail him little, especially as all the crew would turn against him. But supposing he put on the missionary's clothes? The suggestion was a good one. Almost before he had time to know what he was doing, he had taken action—the action that was to turn him into a different person.

It is always one minute that decides our lives for us.

He changed his clothes rapidly. Glisson and he ran fairly of a size; but what was more important still, the missionary's kit was of a rough-and-ready make which rendered fit unimportant. His garments were not what in temperate climates we should regard as a strictly clerical garb, it is true; a white flannel shirt, with a red cross embroidered on it, and a pair of flannel trousers—that was Glisson's simple uniform. But at any rate they were quite unlike Tom's sailor costume, which would have stamped him at once as belonging to the crew of the John Wesley.

He thrust his hand in his pocket, and drew out a worn leather case. It contained a few official letters, addressed to the Rev. Cecil Glisson, Temuka, with some other papers which he had not time at the moment to examine. Then he stuck the Greek Testament into the other pocket, and sat down on a bunk, to await in silence the next development. Naturally, after what he had seen, he was trembling with excitement; but he tried to calm himself and to expect the gunboat.

Another gun went off. The John Wesley lay to, in the trough of the waves. Night was rushing on the sea with tropical rapidity. Below, all was dark. Presently, he heard noises above, noises that sounded like hurried consultation. Next, a boat shimmered quickly past the port-hole by his side. They were lowering it from the davits. In it, he could just make out the dim heads of Ford and Hemmings and some dozen others. He guessed then what was happening. Terrified at the last moment, they were abandoning the John Wesley, and hurrying to seek their fate on the open Pacific. Perhaps some of the sailors had shown a disposition at the last moment to turn Queen's evidence. He thought so afterward. But just at that second, he thought no more about anything. For—r'r'r'—a sudden explosion resounded in his ears. The ship shook from stem to stern. He was dimly aware that Ford had tried to blow up the steamer. That was all he knew. The explosion stunned him. He closed his eyes, with a consciousness of having been violently hit on the forehead by some flying fragment. And in that moment of unconsciousness, so far as the rest of the world was concerned, Tom Pringle faded for ever from existence.

When he came to again, he had changed his personality. He was no longer himself, but Cecil Glisson.

CHAPTER VI.

THE OTHER SIDE OF IT.

THE few breathless minutes that Tom had employed in tremulously changing his clothes down below for Glisson's were a time of wild haste and sudden consternation on deck for the other occupants of the John Wesley. As the gunboat approached, steaming ominously on, an embodied representative of the British empire, their courage began to fail them. Civilisation and law stared at them from her muzzles. They had murdered the blackfellows without a second's compunction, and now, it occurred to them that they had done it in vain. For they had a traitor on board. That man Pringle, if he chose, might round and peach on them.

"I reckon we ought to shoot him," Hemmings suggested calmly, as Tom disappeared down the ladder like a rabbit to its burrow.

"Can't shoot without making a mess," the skipper answered hurriedly. "If they board us, they'll search us; and if they search us and find blood on the decks, there'll be the devil to pay; they'll carry us off to Sydney and try us all for piracy."

"That's so," Hemmings admitted. "It's a bad look-out either way."

"We'd ought to have chucked him over at first with the nigs," Bully Ford continued, glancing round him for support. "That's the only safe way of dealing with a chap who turns traitor."

He said it tentatively, for he knew it was a question whether his crew would obey if he gave such an order. They were ready enough, it is true, to drop blackfellows overboard, in case of emergency; blackfellows are cargo—so much "stock" for the market, to be flung away when it becomes necessary to lighten ship, like any other form of merchandise. But a white man— that was different. *He* was one of themselves, a fellow sailor and a fellow creature; and if once Bully Ford began flinging white men overboard, nobody could tell how soon his own turn might come; it was a dangerous precedent.

So no one responded.

"Shall we chuck him?" the skipper asked in a low voice of Hemmings.

Hemmings cleared his throat. "It's pretty dangerous now," he answered slowly. "She's drawing too near. They've got an eye on us through their glasses; if they happen to see us chuck anything alive, it'll be all the worse for us."

"I'll risk it!" the skipper answered, making up his mind quick. "It's growing dark now, and we could chuck him to leeward next time she lurches——" he paused, and looked significantly at the angry water.

Hemmings pursed his lips. "They'll refuse," he answered low. "They won't chuck a white man."

The skipper turned to two of the sailors. "Fetch up Pringle," he said calmly, in an authoritative voice. "I'm a-going to chuck him."

The men stared at him stonily. "No you don't," one of them answered. "Not with a gunboat bearing down on us. I've had enough of you, Bully Ford, and I tell you so, flat. If you try on that game, I turn Queen's evidence."

Without another word, Bully Ford drew his revolver. "You mean it?" he asked, covering the man.

Quick as lightning, the sailor had whipped out a revolver-in return. "Aye, I mean it," he answered, pointing the muzzle at the skipper. "Take care of yourself, Bully Ford! It's rope, or bullet!"

Bully Ford sprang back. He eyed the other

sailor, who had not yet spoken. In his silent face, he read the same resolution. A second hand went up, and two revolvers covered him. The skipper was a resolute man, making his mind up easily. He saw the game was played. "Lower a boat!" he cried to Hemmings. "There's traitors about! Man her, those of you who are with me! Better run for it than cave in! It's the mercy of the sea, or to be hanged at Sydney!"

Swiftly, silently, with the sudden throbbing consciousness of a great emergency, the sailors who were loyal to the cause of piracy lowered the boat and manned her. It was a hurried moment. Ford and Hemmings stepped into her first. The sea ran high, but they lowered her all the same and put her off successfully. Till the last second, Ford kept his revolver pointed at the two recalcitrant sailors who had refused to chuck Tom Pringle overboard. Then, as the boat rose once on the curling crest of the wave, he took aim steadily.

"What are you doing?" Hemmings asked, seizing the skipper's arm.

"Let me go," the skipper cried, shaking it free and firing. "Do you think I always told you chaps everything on the John Wesley? I'm a-going to blow her up! I've a powder reserve, —and gun-cotton!"

He fired with a steady hand, aiming straight at a particular spot between decks on the John Wesley. The shot took effect. A white puff of smoke rose almost instantly, where the bullet struck, in a huge dense column. Then came a terrible thud; a throb thrilled through the water. The hull reeled: the air trembled. As the smoke cleared away, the place where the two sailors had stood was vacant. Only a mangled limb or two, seen vaguely through the gloom, represented what had been two human lives one moment earlier.

Ford glanced at the hull through the dusk. " Hasn't sunk her! " he muttered with a slight tinge of regret. " But it's killed those beggars, any way! And the other skunk, too, I hope. Well, we're in for it, now, boys: civilisation's all over: there's nothing left us but to try our luck with the savages in the Islands! "

And the boat rowed off through the gathering dusk, before a rising wind, away from the explosion and the pursuing gunboat.

It had all been so rapid, indeed, that half the sailors in the boat hardly realised what was happening, till they found themselves alone in the dark Pacific, a crew of proscribed pirates, rowing off for dear life in an open gig, between the devil and the deep sea—an angry gunboat behind, a stormy ocean in front, and Bully Ford at the stern to steer them to perdition.

One thought was uppermost in every man's breast; one voice alone uttered it. "It's done now, and there's no help for it; but if only I'd knowed, I'm blessed if I'd have started with Bully Ford for the Islands. I'd rather have faced it out, and stood my chance for my life at Sydney."

CHAPTER VII

LAW AND ORDER.

Captain Peachey, of H. M. S. Avenger, stood on deck with his Navigating Lieutenant. " By Jove, Byers," he exclaimed, taking a good look through the telescope, " it's that rascal Bully Ford, in the John Wesley! "

" And we've caught him red-handed? "

" Red-handed? yes. It's my belief, he's chucking his blackfellows overboard to prevent our finding them! "

" Another shot across his bows, sir? " the officer beyond enquired.

" No! That one has brought him to. He'll have to wait now till we come within hailing distance."

The Avenger steamed on, till she was almost alongside the slaver. Then in the dusk the Captain saw strange proceedings aboard. " Hang me," he cried again, " if I don't believe they're going to abandon her! "

" They daren't, on such a night, and five hundred miles from the nearest island."

" Bully Ford would dare anything. Yes, they're putting out boats. We must man ours and follow. Hullo, what's that? " And the Captain paused suddenly.

A column of white smoke rose in the gloom from the John Wesley. Then came a loud dull rumbling. They had blown up the steamer.

In an incredibly short time, the Avenger had put out one of her boats, and rowed through the angry sea to the suspicious steamer. They rowed with caution; for where there has been one explosion there may always be another. But no further noise disturbed them. A party boarded her and examined the derelict. They found two or three mangled bodies of sailors close to the explosion, and nothing else alive on deck or near it.

" These fellows must have been sick of their devil's work," the officer in charge said; " they must have threatened to peach; and Bully Ford has had his revenge on them. It's no use trying to follow him on a night like this. But the sea will have them yet. They never can get away alive to the New Hebrides."

" What next, sir? " the quartermaster asked.

" Search her hold, and see if there are blackfellows below. Though no doubt the rogue has chucked them all overboard."

The sailors went below. In a few minutes, a cry from them brought the officer to the companion. "What's up?" he enquired.

"A wounded man, sir; not one of the crew. Has a red cross on his shirt. Looks as if he might be a missionary."

"Bring him up," the officer said.

The sailors came up, bearing a half lifeless body between them.

The officer bent over it and searched its pockets. "A Greek Testament!" he exclaimed. "You don't expect to find Greek Testaments on a Labour vessel! And a letter-case too! Let's see. 'The Rev. Cecil Glisson, Temuka, by occasion, via Sydney.' Must be a missionary. What the dickens was a missionary doing in this lot, though, I wonder. He can't have been their chaplain. Here's his ordination lines—the Archbishop of Canterbury. Well, they've blown *him* up as well. Lower him gently, boys; lower him gently."

They lowered Tom into the boat, and rowed him back to the Avenger. A crew was put in the John Wesley, to carry her safe to Sydney; and Tom, no longer Tom, was taken cautiously down to a berth in the gunboat.

He lay insensible for two days, for a splinter had struck him on the temple and wounded him badly.

When he came to again, the doctor on the Avenger forbade him to talk for awhile. But he treated him as a missionary. Tom did not even have to tell a lie upon the matter. Nobody questioned him. They took it for granted he was Cecil Glisson. The clothes, the letter-case, the ordination papers, the Greek Testament, all told the same story. It never even occurred to the officers to doubt him. Tom drank his beef tea and held his peace prudently. After all, it was only till they landed at Sydney. Once safe ashore, he could disappear in the crowd, and find a berth on some other ship either there or at Melbourne.

He did not yet realise how hard it is to disappear in a crowd, when once you have done anything to attract attention. Tom Pringle, the unknown Canadian sailor, could vanish into space, and no one would miss him; but Cecil Glisson, the missionary from Temuka, was a marked man; his movements would be chronicled; he could no more vanish unobserved than a prince of the house royal.

As he began to mend, indeed, the ship's officers questioned him about details of his capture. The ship's doctor, on the other hand, counselled quiet and moderation in talking. Tom was glad of that, for when inquiries grew too hot and answers were dubious, he could plead fatigue and gain time for reflection. "I'll tell you by and bye," he would say, and lie back in the folding chair which they had brought out on deck for the convalescent's use. It was only a temporary deception, just to save his own life and to avoid being included in a charge which would be false in essence. He salved his conscience with the thought that if he told the truth, nobody would believe him, and that to tell a white lie was to serve in the end the real cause of justice.

So he threw himself frankly, for this voyage only, into Glisson's part. He answered everything as if he were the missionary. "The ship was Bully Ford's," he said; "and we knew him of old as a desperate slave-stealer. So, when his vessel hove in sight, I went out in our canoes, with my little band of converts, just to let the man feel he was observed and that his proceedings would be reported. I found he had already captured a body of men and girls who were engaged in a religious dance upon the shore; and I paddled up with my crew to look into the matter. All at once, he fired upon us, wounding several of my men, and myself slightly. Then he took me on board, I believe with the intention of letting me die there; but one of his sailors, who was blown up, poor fellow, as well as I can judge, nursed me most carefully, and I was getting convalescent when the Avenger came in sight. Then Ford horrified me by flinging all the stock, as he called it, overboard; and while I was waiting for my turn to come, this explosion occurred; and that's practically all I know about the matter."

" He shall be caught and hanged," the Captain said, " if the Avenger can catch him. He's the worst rogue unhung on the South Pacific! "

Which was saying a great deal as those days went among the Islands.

But the Avenger never found him. Whether the boats foundered in the high seas, or whether they came to shore in one or other of the remoter archipelagoes, was never known. But traders to the Caroline Islands will sometimes tell you that a grey-haired old beach-comber, with three brown families, who is suspected of having tasted human flesh, and is universally known as Cannibal Dick, is really Bully Ford, in the lowest stage of drunken degradation. The story goes that he shot and ate his last companion, and landed, half dead, after many weeks of exposure, at the harbour of Ponapé.

CHAPTER VIII.

A GENTLEMAN AGAIN.

IT was a relief to Tom when after five days'
sail they sighted the Macquarie lighthouse at
the mouth of Sydney Harbour. For now, he said
to himself, he would be able to shuffle off this
false personality which he had unwillingly assumed, and be once more plain Tom Pringle.
" The Reverend " did not suit him. As they
passed between the Heads into that magnificent
port—the most beautiful in the world—Tom was
little engaged in observing the bold and rocky
shore, the fantastic hills, the luxuriant vegeta-
tion of Australian shrubs and orange-trees and
bananas. His mind was wholly occupied with the
consoling thought that he had fairly escaped the
peril of being numbered among the pirates, and
could now disappear into his primitive obscurity.

Still, he was invalided as yet, and unable to
move. He suggested to his kind hosts on board
the Avenger that a few days' stay at the hospital
might be necessary. But the Captain pooh-

poohed the idea. "Preposterous," he said; "preposterous! Why, the Sydney people wouldn't even dream of it. As soon as they know who you are, bless you, they'll be delighted to take you in. One or other of the parsons in the town is sure to annex you. They're the most hospitable set in the world, the Sydney folk. They would feel it a slight on the fame of their hospitality if you ventured to suggest going into a common hospital."

"But I prefer to be independent," Tom said, making a feeble resistance. "I'm a rough South Sea Island missionary, unaccustomed to towns, and I have no clothes with me but those I stand up in: I should get on much better among my blackfellows at Temuka than in parson's dress in a Sydney drawing-room."

"Nonsense," the Captain answered, good-humouredly. "A clergyman is a clergyman, and must behave as sich. He's none the worse for going out like a man to risk his life among savages. I don't say as a rule I'm fond of missionaries, Glisson—seen a deal too many of them—they're always giving us trouble on the Pacific stations: but hang it all, when a man *is* a man, as you are, and goes among such rough savages as those Temuka fellows, prepared to die for what he believes the truth—whether it's true or isn't

—why, I don't see how one can help liking and admiring him."

Tom winced a little. This was hard to endure. To be modest under praise for what you have never done is trying to the nerves. But he consoled himself by thinking it was only for a time, and he would soon escape from it.

" Besides," the Captain went on, " you've got no precious parson nonsense about you. You're a Man—that's what I like about you. You can laugh and talk and join in with the rest of us. If a sailor like myself happens accidentally to let drop an occasional *damn*, you don't pull a long face over it as if you thought he was straight on the road to perdition. I admire a parson who can fight for his beliefs, but doesn't want to thrust them down other people's throats. Leave your quarters to me, Glisson: when we get into port, I'll take jolly good care you're properly looked after by a decent sort of family."

This was just what Tom didn't want; but he dared not say nay. He only murmured feebly: " But I've got no clothes except these that I wear. And I've got no money. Everything I had is left at Temuka."

" All the more reason you should be taken in and looked after by some good Samaritan. If you landed with your pocket full of money, and a clean white choker, you could go at once to the best hotel in Sydney. But, hang it all, if people won't look after a wounded parson, who's been blown up by slavers because he tried to take care of his own people, and who returns to civilisation with a shirt to his back and nothing else much to brag about—what's our Christianity good for, I wonder? Just you leave that to me. *I'll* take care that Sydney doesn't lose its reputation for hospitality."

Tom winced again. These laudations hurt him. But he was forced to submit. He must keep up this farce till he was well enough to move, and could run away by rail or sea to Melbourne. There, he would have a chance of picking up a vessel.

Captain Peachey was quite right in his prognostication. As soon as all Sydney knew that a wounded missionary from the South Seas was aboard the Avenger, and that he had come aboard from an abandoned and blown up Labour vessel with nothing in the world save the clothes he wore, all Sydney was eager to show him its harbour and its hospitality—those being in point of fact the two things on which proud Sydney most especially prides itself. Half-a-dozen clergymen in the town were eager to put him up. Tom, seeing there was nothing else for it, selected from among them the one who seemed to him least obtrusively clerical. This was a certain Mr. Strong, a rector in the town, with a pleasant house in one of the most fashionable suburbs. Almost before he had realised the step he was taking, he found himself lifted into a comfortable carriage, and driven slowly through the streets to his host's home by the Parramatta river.

Two things buoyed him up at this trying moment. He had never been at Sydney before; and he knew from Cecil Glisson's own lips that the dead man he was half innocently personating had never been there either. So the chance of meeting any one who could detect the deception either way—who could say with confidence " This is Tom Pringle," or " This is not Cecil Glisson " —was in so far lessened.

The carriage drew up at a pretty suburban house, ringed round by a verandah, and covered with bright creepers. A girl of twenty stood waiting at the door. " Olive, my dear," his host said, " *this* is Mr. Glisson."

By this time, Tom was beginning to get sick of it. His first impulse was to cry out: " Oh, no, it isn't; it's only Tom Pringle, a sailor out of work, from the steamer John Wesley." But two things restrained him. One was the fear that if he told the truth he might be indicted as one of a gang of sea murderers; the other was the apparently irrelevant fact that Olive Strong was distinctly pretty.

·A serious question in the history of orders in the English Church hung ultimately on Olive Strong's appearance that moment. Had she been less attractive, the doubt as to the validity of ordinations in the diocese of Dorchester which afterwards agitated the soul of a bishop might never have arisen.

Tom looked at her shyly. Olive Strong was a vigorous, well-built girl, of what we should nowadays call the lawn-tennis-playing type, but which was rarer in those days, lawn-tennis not having yet been invented. She was tall, after the frequent Australian fashion, and very supplely knit; her movements made a pleasing compromise between grace and strength; her step was light, but her poise was self-confident with the just self-confidence of youth, health, and vigour, in a beautiful woman's body. That was Tom's first impression: what he noticed most of all as he looked at her that moment was this abundant sense of life and fitness. Olive Strong was, above everything else, a capable woman.

He looked again, and saw next that his host's daughter was also pretty. Not violently, obtrusively, aggressively pretty; certainly not pretty in the common acceptation, with prettiness of the coloured chocolate-box order. Quiet strength of character gave the key-note to her face; she was pretty with the prettiness that is an index of effectiveness. Till then, Tom had always vaguely admired, after the fashion of very young men, the mere pink-and-white complexion, the fluffy hair, the somewhat hot-house beauty of the artificial young woman. He had admired small hands, enclosed in still smaller dainty kid gloves; small feet, jammed close in tight high-heeled boots; a waist, too narrow for the organs it should contain, and still further cramped by the art of the corset-maker. He had admired that soft white skin which comes of insufficient exercise and lack of exposure to healthy sun and air; he had admired in one word what is considered "feminine," but what is really a mere product of the boudoir and the hairdresser's shop, —violet powder, bloom of Ninon, bandoline, and lip-salve.

Admired it from afar, for the most part, of course, for Tom's own position as a common sailor had not allowed him of late years to see much more of such women than a passing glimpse in a street when he was in port for a fortnight. Still, that was hitherto his ideal—the laced and bandaged woman of the fashion-plate, the blanched and etiolated product of an exotic culture.

He gazed at Olive Strong, and felt his notions undergo a sudden expansion, an instantaneous reversal. For Olive was quite other than this preconceived model, yet she struck him at sight as far more truly beautiful than any other girl he had ever yet hit upon. Her skin was brown, a rich transparent creamy brown, not unburnt by the strong sun of the southern heavens. But in spite of its brownness, the bright colour on her cheek glowed through it with a red flush, which deepened somewhat as Tom's eyes fixed themselves upon hers for a moment with too frank a glance. He had to recall his clericalism and curb his eagerness for a second. Then the sailor in him overcame the pretended parson, and he gazed back once more, to note that Olive had quietly beautiful eyes—not eyes of tropical splendour or of arch coquetry, like the ladies of the stage whom he had most admired, but calm, serene, strong, able eyes, eyes that gave assurance of steadfastness and capacity. Her features might not seem very delicately moulded to an unobservant eye; they were the features of a good woman and a powerful character rather than those of a professed beauty. Yet when Tom looked closer, he saw with the rapid intuition of a man for the help that is meet for him that they were really modelled with underlying firmness and elusive delicacy. Even at a first glance, he noticed in particular a certain dainty cutting away of the lid of the nostrils, which gave a singular quiver to her charming smile, and reminded him somehow of a high-bred Arab. Taken as a whole, Olive Strong was not fair to outer view with the fairness that would take the most casual observer; but Tom Pringle, who had more in him than he himself suspected, saw at once that she possessed a deeper and a more perfect type of beauty than any that he had ever yet learned to think beautiful.

He was sorry as he gazed at her that he was *not* a missionary.

What had ailed him to run away to sea and turn common sailor? That was his real great error. After all, he was better born and better bred than Glisson. But he had thrown away his chances for a boyish freak; and though he loved the sea, and had never before complained of it, it occurred to him now with a pang of regret that he had made it impossible for himself ever to marry a girl of the same class and stamp as Olive.

It is so delightful to find oneself with " a real lady."

Fully to realise what those hackneyed words mean, however, you must have lived, like Tom, for some years as a common sailor.

Olive stood on the step of the door and welcomed him. "You must make yourself quite at home," she said, with that quivering smile. "I'm accustomed to invalids, Mr. Glisson, and I'm so very glad you were able to come to us. Not too quick up the steps—we know how you must have been shaken. Captain Peachey told Papa what the Avenger's doctor said—the real wonder was that you should have escaped at all, when the men by your side were killed in the explosion."

"Oh, I feel all right now," Tom answered—and, to do him justice, at that moment he did. "I can walk quite well; it's only my head that gives me any trouble."

Olive led him to a long wicker chair on the verandah. A passion-flower draped it in lithe festoons. "You'd better sit here awhile," she said, "and rest, before you go to your room. The doctor told us we mustn't let you exert yourself at all for some days. You must have perfect quiet."

Perfect quiet! And in such society! With his heart beating ten extra beats per minute! Tom began to feel more wretched and more guilty than ever. Oh, why had he consented to himself to begin this deception? He had half a mind even now to brazen it all out, and declare himself a member of the crew of pirates. Fancy living for some days in the bosom of a family, with this charming girl, and palming oneself off as a pious missionary! Could he keep it up, he wondered, —he, the most careless and happy-go-lucky of sailors. And even if he could, how heartily he must despise himself!

"Oh, I dare say by to-morrow or next day I shall be well enough to—to think about getting back," Tom began, growing hot. Then, seeing the look of surprise on Olive's face, he added quickly, "Of course I mustn't presume to trespass one day longer than is necessary on your kind hospitality."

"Why not?" Olive asked, astonished at this strange haste. "We're delighted to see you. And then, we sympathise so much with your work, you see. I think it so brave of you to go and risk your life like that, all for a pure idea, among those dreadful savages. Captain Peachey told Papa you almost gave up your own safety for your people—and you were taken, defending them, by those horrid slavers. Of course one ought to be glad one's allowed to do anything for those who will do so much for others."

Tom's face was fiery hot. This was more

than he could endure. "I—I have done nothing," he answered. "Nothing, nothing at all, I assure you. I'm afraid you misunderstand. I—I couldn't help being taken prisoner." Then a certain sense of loyalty to poor dead Glisson closed his lips once more. It was of Glisson she was speaking, not of his own doings. How could he dissociate the tangled personalities? how venture to make light of that brave fellow's acts? For though he had only been a few days in Glisson's company on the John Wesley, he had learned to appreciate and admire to the full the strength and devotion of that simple, manly, single-hearted young Englishman.

He grew hotter and redder still as he thought of this treachery. And Olive, who saw it, put it all down to the brave young missionary's excessive modesty. His very discomfiture told in his favour. The more he floundered, the better she thought of him.

CHAPTER IX.

ENTANGLEMENT.

THREE days later, the Rev. Cecil Glisson, *alias* Tom Pringle, sat on the verandah of the Strongs' house on the Parramatta River, looking out with dazed eyes towards the beautiful harbour. He was a Reverend indeed: in the clothes which he wore, Tom hardly knew himself. For there he sat, rigged out in a complete suit of black clerical broadcloth, hastily made to measure by the best tailor in Sydney. It was in vain that he had protested on four different grounds, personal, economical, moral, and sartorial, against this complete transformation of his outer man: his host maintained that a clergyman in Sydney must dress as Sydney does: he must wear the accepted clerical clothes of a civilised parish: and Tom, after fighting a losing battle all along the line, had finally retired from the contest, discomfited. The financial argument was a strong one. He declared he had no means to pay for his new suit, having arrived in Sydney without a penny to bless himself: Mr. Strong replied that as local secretary of the Church of England Missionary Society it was *his* duty to see to the proper clothing of shipwrecked or destitute missionaries, and that Tom must submit to his superior officer. Then Tom urged feebly that he could never wear it when he returned to Temuka; to which Mr. Strong rejoined that his return to Temuka was a problematical event, after the harm inflicted upon him by the fight and the explosion. "We like enthusiasm," he said, smiling; "but we don't desire our missionaries to court martyrdom too easily; the palm should be won, not snatched; and *you* want to snatch it." Tom blushed uneasily again; in point of fact, no man on earth felt less anxious for martyrdom than he did. He relapsed into silence, and allowed himself to be passively measured for his clerical suit without further remonstrance.

And now, the hateful black things had come home in due course, and Tom found himself, to his own intense discomfort, masquerading in that very uncongenial costume before Olive Strong on her own verandah.

"I don't even know how to wear them, Miss Strong," he said apologetically, conscious of his own awkwardness—for a clerical suit is not precisely adapted to the habits and attitudes of the British sailor. "You see—" he paused again, for at heart he was a tolerably honest young man, and he shrank from lying—" at Temuka, I never wore them. In the Islands, of course, we go about always in nothing but flannels. And I've lived so long in rough places now that I've almost forgotten how to be civilised."

"I like you *best* in your flannel shirt and red cross," Olive answered with naïve confidence.

Tom fingered his moustache nervously: he was glad of that; for in the flannel shirt he was at least himself. And he admired Olive intensely: so he was pleased she preferred him in a rougher garb. Indeed, it began to strike him that after three or four days in that comfortable home with that bright young girl, it would be hard to go back again to the coarse life of the forecastle. He remembered all at once that he had been brought up a gentleman.

"One feels so much more at home in flannels," he went on. "I really don't believe I could ever get used to these stiff black things. They run counter to my ideas. I'm a man of adventure. I don't love civilisation."

"I suppose you've never worn a white tie —not since you were first ordained," Olive suggested. "You went straight out from ordination to Temuka, didn't you?" ·

She was right as to Glisson. Glisson had told him so much; but still, why did she know it? "How did you find that out?" Tom asked, looking up quickly.

The colour deepened on the dark cheek. "I saw it in the Missionary Record," she answered after a conscious pause.

Then she had hunted him up in it. Or hunted up Glisson—which? This confusion of persons was growing most unpleasant. Once more, for a second, Tom was minded to make a clean breast of it and cry out with fervour: "I am no parson, no missionary, but plain Tom Pringle!" Then he bethought him of what the Sydney papers were saying; if Bully Ford and his crew could only be caught, not one man of them should be allowed to escape hanging. And this first false step only made things worse. Had he told the truth at first, he might have run some chance of being believed, by virtue of his frankness; now that he had complicated matters by passively accepting Cecil Glisson's personality, there was nothing left but to go through with it boldly.

He saved himself by a prevarication. "The Missionary Record is quite right," he said. This committed him to nothing. For the Missionary Record declared that Cecil Glisson had gone out from his ordination straight to Temuka; and in declaring so much, the Missionary Record had merely confirmed what Cecil Glisson himself had told him.

He paused a moment. He was a very poor liar. Then he added: "I shall be glad to get them off again. Of course, when I go back to the Islands, I shall never wear them. It seems wasteful to have bought them for so short a visit."

Olive Strong fixed her eyes on him. "So short a visit!" she repeated. "Why, how long do you think you will stop at Sydney?"

Tom was aware with a thrill that she asked it almost anxiously. Then he remembered once more, with a pang of disillusion, that her anxiety was all for Cecil Glisson. And yet!—And yet, it was he himself, not Cecil Glisson, that she saw before her. If she was interested in anybody, it was surely himself. The disentanglement of the personalities grew each moment more difficult.

"As soon as I am well enough, I think I *ought* to go back," he answered slowly.

"Oh, Mr. Glisson!"

She said no more than that, but then, she looked at him. Tom felt her eyes go through and through him. He wriggled uncomfortably in his stiff new suit. He was aware that this evident eagerness to run away was a poor return for the Strongs' marked kindness. Was ever fellow placed in a more awkward predicament? He had to choose between rude ingratitude on the one side, and continued deception on the other. Which of the two should it be? He looked hard at Olive's face,—and deception carried it.

"Well, everybody at Sydney has been so kind," he said evasively, "that of course I should *like* to stop as long as possible; on some accounts,"—his eye met hers—"I should like to stop . . . for an indefinite period. But then—I have duties; my duties call me." His face was now in a fine red glow. He paused, and felt himself a consummate hypocrite.

Olive looked up sharply. "But you're not going back to Temuka?" she said, with a distinct flutter.

Tom's heart, like the Homeric hero's, stood divided two ways within him. As Tom Pringle, he felt inclined to say: "Oh, certainly not;" as Cecil Glisson, he felt constrained to affect a professional interest in the well-being of the natives. He took refuge once more in a safe generality. "A man mustn't be daunted by one first disappointment," he answered, vaguely; "by one first difficulty. To put one's hand to the plough and then turn back is bad. Apart from anything else, it shows lack of courage."

"I don't think anybody would suspect *you* of want of courage," Olive answered with conviction. And once more Tom coloured. The remark was true enough, even as applied to himself; for Tom had the usual endowment of the British sailor in that respect; he was by no means a coward: but he knew the praise was intended for Glisson, and it made him uncomfortable. Olive noticed his blush, and thought all the better of him for it. "He's as modest as he's brave," she said to herself admiringly. As a rule, to be sure, she was not attracted by curates; but this bronzed and weather-beaten young missionary (as she naturally thought him), with his frank sailor face and his shy sailor manners, was only a parson by the accident of orders. In essence she felt— and felt more truly than she knew—he was of the genus explorer, a daring young fellow who took his life in his hands, and accepted mission work with the eager delight of a boy in a dangerous adventure. She noticed, indeed, that when he talked of his own life (which was seldom) he dwelt little on professional details, but spoke much of the sea, the fight with the Labour vessel, the delights of roughing it, the savagery of the natives. Olive had lived long enough in a clerical family to be just a trifle sick of the slang of parochialism; but this South Sea Island parson in the flannel shirt seemed to her a totally new species—and no wonder.

"I don't think you *ought* to go back," she interposed after a pause. "You know now how dangerous it is. Even if you don't mind for yourself, you should consider others—your mother, for instance, or your sisters."

"I have no mother," Tom answered, turning towards her as he spoke, and catching his neck on that horrid round collar. "She died years ago, my dear good mother. And I never had a sister." Which was true, every word of it, both of himself and the man he personated. Then he prevaricated again. "If you looked up the name of Glisson in the Missionary Record," he added, "didn't it mention that the fellow came out of a Liverpool orphanage?"

"It did," Olive replied, admiring him still more for his honest frankness and complete absence of snobbery. "But then, I thought perhaps that might only mean that you had lost your father."

"I have lost both parents," Tom answered, "and I was an only son." Which again was equally true of himself and of Glisson. Then he plunged once more. "I think," he went on, the thought really occurring to him on the spur of the moment, "only people without home ties ought ever to undertake missionary work. It's too dangerous for men with mothers and sisters—it puts too great a strain on their affections. Apart from the possibilities of being killed and eaten, just think what torture it must be for a mother who loves one to wait months together without the chance of a letter—and with all the terrors of a tropical climate and the caprices of savages vividly before her mind all the time in the night watches."

"You're quite right," Olive answered. "I never thought of that before. But I see it now. It must be really terrible. . . . Yet *some* missionaries even take their wives out with them."

"And have children born to them in the Islands; yes; they do: but do you think it is right, it is fair to a woman? *I* don't. A man may risk his own life if he likes, especially in a good cause; it's his own to chuck away, his own to gamble with—I mean, to use for what he thinks the highest purpose." (Very difficult for a sailor to assume all at once this new professional manner!) "But his wife's and his children's,—no! There are dangers to which no man should expose a woman—least of all a woman he loves. And his little children! Do you remember how those missionaries' families were massacred and tortured in Madagascar? It makes me feel that no man should ever take a wife with him on such an expedition." And he shuffled in his clothes, for the collar galled him.

Olive paused to consider. "I think you're right," she said at last,—"as a matter of principle, for the man. And yet—it's very hard that men who are exposed to such risks should not be cheered and encouraged by the consolation of a wife's care, a wife's help, a wife's sympathy."

After that, there was a long pause. Tom spent it in reflecting that if he *were* a missionary, and he *had* a chance of winning such a girl as Olive, he would certainly *not* take her to Temuka, to be cooked and eaten. It was all very well to talk about putting one's hand to the plough and not looking back; for a celibate clergy, that was an excellent rule. A monk might stick to it. But if you were going to marry a wife like Olive —hang it all, you ought to govern yourself accordingly, and make a home fit for her. There could be no great merit in marrying a wife, and exposing her to risks too horrible to contemplate. Such vicarious martyrdom in no way suited Tom's sailor nature.

As for Olive, she spent the same moments in

reflecting that Mr. Glisson was a charming young man,—so simple, so brave, so candid, so honest; and that it was a pity he thought of going back to Temuka—especially if he meant to go alone, and thought it positively wrong to take a wife out with him. She certainly wouldn't care to live at Temuka herself; the isolation and the danger must both be terrible: and if a young man such as Mr. Glisson were to ask her to marry him—which of course was improbable—she would much prefer he should make her a home in New South Wales or in England. Theoretically, she was an ardent supporter of foreign missions—it was her duty as her father's daughter to be so; but practically and personally she felt that not every one is called to this difficult work, and that, unless you have a call, it would be foolish to embark in it. Which showed Olive's good sense; for no more people are fitted to be missionaries than to be scientific explorers; and a missionary who is not to the manner born makes his own life wretched, without doing much good to anybody else's.

Glisson, the real Glisson, *was* a missionary born. He had that ardent love of universal humanity, black, white, or brown, which is essential to success in his chosen calling: and he had also that buoyant hope, that unfailing energy which alone can sustain a man through the disappointments and failures of a life spent in trying to raise lower natures to a height far above them. He had the enthusiasm of humanity. Tom, who was only an amiable and adventurous young sailor, felt conscious how difficult it was for him to sustain the part of such a fervent apostle. Fortunately, he thought to himself, he had only to do it for a few days longer, and then, he could get away and be once more a mere boisterous British sailor.

In which case, of course, he must say good-bye, for ever, to Olive.

That was a painful consequence of his half-unwilling deception. For he began to be aware that in those few short days Olive had come to mean a great deal to him.

CHAPTER X.

ACCIDENT, I hold, is answerable for much in most human lives; it was answerable for almost everything in Tom Pringle's. When he first decided to change his clothes hurriedly for Cecil Glisson's in the cabin of the John Wesley, on that critical evening, he had certainly no deeper intention than to escape for the moment from an awkward predicament into which chance had led him. He had taken a berth on the Labour vessel without the faintest idea of the true nature of the trade in which she was engaged; that first unfortunate step had involved his taking an unwilling part in the fight and the capture of the blackfellows.

When he saw the Avenger bearing down upon Bully Ford, he had had no thought beyond that of putting himself visibly on the right side, and disclaiming all share in the John Wesley's nefarious proceedings. Most assuredly he had not anticipated masquerading for a whole week in clerical dress as the dead man's representative. As soon as he discovered into what difficulties this one false step had landed him, his sole anxiety was next to get free from the coils of his deception. He desired to leave Sydney as early as possible; he wanted to find some homeward-bound ship on which he could bury himself once more in his native obscurity. Meanwhile, he had a sense that he was acting in private theatricals, dressed up for the singularly uncongenial part of an English curate.

But the stars in their courses fought against Tom Pringle, and slowly compelled him to a continued deception. He was not well enough to go out for a week after he reached Sydney. As soon as he could move with safety, he determined in his own soul that he would slink away in Glisson's red-cross shirt; sell his uncomfortable new black parson suit for what it would fetch at a marine store dealer's; buy such other clothes as he could obtain with the money; and then sign articles for any voyage to any port on earth, provided only he could at once shuffle off this uncomfortable personality which his own rash act had foolishly thrust upon him.

Here again, however, the fates were unpropitious. On the morning when he confidently hoped to get away, he had a relapse, no doubt through nervous anxiety, and had to yield himself up once more to Olive's nursing. And Olive's nursing was always so delightful that he felt in his heart he could be only half sorry for it. Of course, he would not allow himself to *fall in love* with that girl. It would be madness—under the circumstances: nay, worse, it would be dishonourable. He was only a common sailor, however well born—for his father had been a gentleman; and if Olive showed some slight liking for him, no doubt that was only because she thought he was Cecil Glisson. Though to be sure, if it came to that, is it not rather the concrete man now and here before a girl that she falls in love with, not his name or antecedents? If you fall in love, do you not fall in love with a person rather than with a profession? These were pregnant questions. Still, it was absurd in any case for him to think about Olive. And if Olive thought about him, his clear duty as a man of honour was to pretend to ignore it. Indeed, what else could he do? It would be useless to win Olive's heart as the Reverend Cecil Glisson, and then have to confess he was plain Tom Pringle, able-bodied mariner, without a penny in the world, and with not the faintest chance of ever supporting a wife of her quality.

Meanwhile, to make things worse, Sydney

did not allow the supposed parson to rest at peace in his convalescence. They had caught a hero, and they meant to lionize him. On the Thursday of that week, two clergymen called, with Mr. Strong to back them up, and made the unexpected, the wholly incredible request that Tom would preach in aid of the Mission Fund to the South Seas on Sunday.

Tom preach! He had never even dreamt of that appalling possibility. It was too absurd. His horror and consternation showed themselves legibly on his face. Preach—in a church! Oh, dear saints, deliver us!

" Not at all," his host said blandly—for he was a suave parson. " We don't want a set sermon, Glisson. What our people would like best to hear is a plain account in simple language of your own mission."

Temuka indeed! Where he had spent one wild day! What on earth could he tell them of it?

There is a legal and moral maxim that no one becomes of a sudden a blackguard—nemo repente fit turpissimus. And Tom did not descend at once into the lowest depths of duplicity. I tell you all this, at some length, because, unless I told you step by step how the great deception arose, you would think more hardly of him than the circumstances justify. You would set him down, *sans phrase*, as an unmitigated scoundrel; when, as a matter of fact, he was to some extent merely the victim of circumstances.

This first naked suggestion that he should clothe himself in a surplice and mount the steps of a pulpit to expound the Word struck his mind, indeed, as a horrible profanity. He did not plot and scheme to personate a clergyman; certainly he did not rush into it with deliberate hypocrisy. On the contrary he drew back from the consequences of his act with genuine fear and unfeigned horror. "Oh, no," he said, taken aback. "I could never dream of preaching." Then, the necessity for keeping up the farce recurred to him, and he added hastily, as an afterthought, "before an educated congregation such as one would have at Sydney." It was only just in time that he remembered to say "congregation" instead of "audience"—the word that had first naturally occurred to him.

Mr. Strong, however, would hear of no refusal. Tom pleaded ill-health. Very well, then; if not this week, why, next. Tom declared he had never preached to a body of English hearers. Oh, that was not what they wanted; they did not care for a discourse full of orthodox doctrine; they would like to have just some plain account of his own work and his strange adventures. Much talking at last wears down all opposition. Overborne by their importunity, Tom consented in the end, for the sake of peace and quiet, reserving in his own soul the silent determination to contract on the fatal day a sudden indisposition.

Olive for her part was much interested in this sermon. "I don't think, Mr. Glisson," she said, "you ought exactly to *preach* to them." She liked and admired her young missionary, and she thought him clever, too; but she doubted whether his cleverness ran in the direction of hortatory discourse. "Why shouldn't you talk to them just as you've talked to us here, about the wickedness of this Labour trade, and the necessity for doing something to put down its horrors?"

"That would hardly be churchy," Tom interposed, very dubiously.

"I don't think the apostles cared much whether things were churchy," Olive answered with common sense. "And I know that's not yourself. At Temuka, I'm sure, you didn't think about churchiness. You were satisfied to be simple. Here, you're filled with the idea that Sydney's a great town, and that what was good enough for Temuka wouldn't be good enough for us.   But I can see you are horrified and indignant at this wicked slave-trading that goes on almost unchecked under our own flag; why don't you just stand up in a pulpit and say so in your own way—tell them what you've told Papa and me here alone in the evenings?   It would be real: it would be genuine.   And it would do more good than a great·many sermons—which you and I know nobody ever listens to."

Tom thought the notion a good one—as far as it went.   He didn't mean to go in for the profanation of preaching in church at all—he must back out of it somehow.   Still, if he *had* to preach, (he, in a clean white surplice!) he really thought he would do as Olive suggested.   While he had nothing particular to say about justification by faith—and he felt himself lamentably weak in that direction—he had a great deal to say about Bully Ford and his proceedings.   What he had seen on the John Wesley had stirred his indignation.   His blood boiled at it.

Queensland pretended it knew nothing of these things: but Queensland was built up on a virtual slave trade.   And then, he reflected that he was now in a sense Cecil Glisson's representative.   A strange feeling of loyalty to the dead · man possessed him.   As long as this miserable deception lasted, and people still believed him to be Cecil Glisson, he ought at least to behave in a way that would bring no discredit upon the ardent young missionary whose place he had usurped. If Glisson were alive, Tom thought, he would certainly go into a Sydney pulpit and preach such and such a sermon.

As he lay awake at night, wondering how he was ever to creep out of this hole into which he had let himself, he thought that sermon all out in his head, just as Glisson would have preached it —just as he would preach it himself if he were a real registered A1 parson. Part of it he made up from his vivid recollection of the stirring things Cecil Glisson had said to him when he lay dying on the John Wesley, filled even in death with that unquenchable enthusiasm of humanity; part of it he supplied from his own experiences on the hateful Labour vessel.

He was almost sorry he couldn't preach such a sermon; it might do much good; more good by many lengths than half the sermons one hears —mere strings of commonplace droned out to order by perfunctory parsons. *He* had something to say, and he thought he could say it. It was a pity, after all, the chance could never occur for him. If he *had* been a parson, how hot he would make it for the smugly respectable Queensland planter!

He thought that sermon all out in every sentence and every epithet. He was not aware of it himself, but, being half Irish by descent, he had the natural Irish gift of eloquence. Going on with his sermon, he worked himself up to a pitch of enthusiasm in the dead hours of the morning. He half rehearsed it to himself in an impassioned undertone. He was enslaved by his own phrases. What a pity he couldn't deliver it as a lecture at least! He found himself carried away by the sense of his own message.

And he *had* a message. He was Cecil Glisson for the moment, with a burning story to tell of wrong and cruelty. If only he could tell it, he felt sure he had the power to make people listen.

He talked of it next day to Olive. *She* listened certainly. She was enthusiastic about the necessity for putting down this vile traffic, and preaching a new crusade. " I believe, Mr. Glisson," she said with confidence, " you would be twice as well employed in opening the eyes of people in Australia and England to the wickedness of this labour trade than in evangelising Temuka. It is a larger work. You would be doing more real service to your people, I'm sure, than by merely teaching. And besides, you wouldn't have to settle down again in the Islands then: and yet you wouldn't feel you were turning back your hand from the plough either!"

Tom was a modest enough young fellow, not apt to suppose such a girl as Olive was likely to care for him; but when he posed as Glisson, he felt at once that a certain new element was imported into the situation. As she said those last words, with a faint flush on the dark cheek, and a slight droop of the downcast eyes, as if half afraid she was showing too obvious an interest in her hearer's welfare, it did occur to Tom as possible that Olive Strong was falling in love, if not with him, at any rate with Cecil Glisson. Now, if you are acting a part, and a woman falls in love with that part you are acting, it is difficult for you to dissever the character from the actor. So Tom felt at that moment. It was a queer conundrum. Supposing Olive Strong was in love with Cecil Glisson, was not Tom the Cecil Glisson Olive Strong was in love with?

From that moment forth, his life became one long attempt both to entangle and to disentangle those two diverse personalities. They puzzled even himself. The Cecil Glisson of the future was an artificial compromise between the real Tom Pringle and the dead missionary of Temuka.

And when Olive said those words, it occurred

to Tom that by doing his best against that iniquitous slave traffic he would in a certain sense be carrying out Cecil Glisson's wishes. Fate rather than deliberate design had forced him into this impersonation of a dead man whom he could not help respecting; surely the way in which he could at any rate do least dishonour to the part he had been driven by accident to assume would be by acting at Cecil Glisson himself would have acted had he been really living.

Tom was turned by circumstances into a complete casuist.

CHAPTER XI.

TOM PLUNGES.

TEMPTATION creeps from point to point. Sunday came at last—that eventful Sunday, which formed the real turning-point in the history of Tom Pringle's half-unwilling deception. Till Sunday, retreat was still always possible; by Monday, it was not: he had raised meanwhile an impassable barrier between the new Cecil Glisson and the old Tom Pringle.

He came down to breakfast half undecided how to act. He still clung to the hope that he might plead indisposition. But as he entered the breakfast-room, with a furtive smile, his host dispelled that illusion by saying at once: "Oh, how much better you look this morning, Glisson! You're a man again, I see. You've picked up wonderfully in our bracing climate. Next to its harbour, Sydney prides itself on its air: it is as good as England after a year or two of the tropics."

"I'm so glad you're so well," Olive went on.

looking up from the tea-tray, where she was occupied as housewife. "We've all set our hearts, you know, upon your undertaking this crusade; and indeed, when you can do it so well, we can none of us imagine why you want to shirk it."

"Too much modesty," her father answered. "But then, modesty is not always an unalloyed virtue. A man should have just confidence in his own powers. However, you're fit enough, Glisson; that's one good point; and I haven't a doubt you will find our people enthusiastic."

What could poor Tom do? He was not ecclesiastical, and the act did not occur to him as a great sacrilege—just then at least; the honest historian is bound to admit that he considered it rather as an awkward social fix, out of which he must extricate himself by a disagreeable piece of solemn masquerading. Yet of one thing he was sure; it was no use now to plead indisposition. As Mr. Strong said, he was fit— undeniably fit. He felt it; he looked it; and he felt he looked it. The fresh air of a temperate country had revived him wonderfully after his illness on the Avenger; and the unwonted luxury of that comfortable home, with the equally unwonted pleasure of a lady's society, had succeeded in making him happy and lively in spite of his anxiety. He was adventurous by nature. If chance thrust this adventure upon him against his will, why, he must embrace it, that was all, and pull himself out of it as well as he was able. Though he *did* draw a line at personating a parson in the very pulpit.

He got through breakfast somehow. How, he hardly knew himself. He crumbled his bread and gulped down his coffee. He was too tremulous even to be conscious of his stiff white choker. After breakfast, Olive spoke to her father in the study for a moment. " He's terribly nervous," she said (and her father, who was a student of human nature, observed for the first time that she spoke of their visitor as " he," not as " Mr. Glisson," as though there were no other *he's* in the world worth considering). " Did you notice that he hardly ate anything, and that he seemed quite frightened? "

" He *is* nervous," her father answered, pulling his clerical tie straight in front of the glass. "But is that to be wondered at? Remember, it is practically his first sermon. He never *preached* at Temuka. He just talked and explained things in a very crude language to a set of savages. I was nervous myself when I preached my first sermon. But *that* was before a bishop, and I was an unknown man; whereas Glisson has the advantage of a congregation entirely predisposed in his favour.”

“ I shall make him take a glass of port in a medicine bottle,” Olive exclaimed, “ and drink it in the vestry just before the sermon.”

“An excellent thing,” her father answered. “*With* an egg beaten up in it. But he will be all right, I’m sure, when once he begins. His heart is in this matter, and therefore he’ll speak well about it.”

At a quarter to eleven, a neighbour’s carriage called for Tom by appointment. As the fatal hour drew nigh, he grew whiter and more terrified. The real seriousness of the step he was taking did not even now appeal to him from the point of view of sacrilege: but he was increasingly conscious of the social ordeal. He drove to church in silence, with trembling knees. He had not felt half so frightened in the jungle at Temuka, when the blackfellows were peppering them from behind the brushwood.

Through the earlier part of the service he sat in a white surplice and a face somewhat whiter. The terror of the task increased upon him each instant. When at length the dreaded moment arrived, he had one last impulse to rise in his place and cry aloud: “ I am not Cecil Glisson; I have been fooling you all: I am only Tom

Pringle, an able-bodied mariner." But he caught Olive's eye, and the sight of her restrained him. The crucial moment went by, and went by for ever. Next instant, in a breathless turmoil, and with legs that scarcely bore him, he felt himself mounting the pulpit stairs, as if by some strange external compulsion, and saw a sea of up-turned faces all looking towards him and waiting.

As he stood there for one second, pausing and drawing breath, it occurred to him all at once that though he had quite decided in his own mind what sort of sermon he should preach, if he had to preach a sermon, the trifling initial formality of a text had entirely escaped him. In an agony of dismay, he opened the big Bible on the rail in front of him; opened it at random, and gave out the first words on which his eye lighted. They happened luckily to be these— "And I, brethren, when I came to you, came not with excellency of speech or wisdom." Tom uttered them mechanically; then he looked at his congregation. A sudden sense of their congruity overcame him. "That is true," he said simply. " I will ask you to listen to me, not for my poor manner of delivering my message, but because I *have* a message to give to the people of Sydney."

After that, he paused again and looked round. Then, conscious of the unique importance of the moment, he dropped his voice suddenly to a colloquial tone and began to tell his hearers, in his homely sailor way, the story of what he had seen on board the John Wesley. He forgot for the moment he was supposed to be Cecil Glisson; but as he spoke impersonally, that lapse did not much matter. He told them how skippers such as Bully Ford, sailing under the British flag, and making that flag hateful to the people of the South Pacific, descended suddenly, like birds of prey that swoop from the sky, upon those beautiful islands. He described with simple but graphic eloquence the harbour of Temuka, its rampart of rock, its palms, its waterfalls. He told them how the white men were armed and trained; how ruthless was their method; how their business was that of organised slave-stealers. He painted in the telling touches of an eye-witness the landing on the white beach; the terror of the first villagers; the toilsome march through the tangled forest; the fierce swoop of onslaught upon the defenceless natives; the seizure and handcuffing of men and women; the swift retreat to the boats; the utter carelessness of life; the treatment of the slaves as though they were bales of merchandise. It was a picture from life: as he spoke, his hearers seemed to see it all before them.

Then, still in an impersonal way, as if he were neither himself nor Cecil Glisson, he described in few words how a missionary living among these people, and anxiously endeavouring to teach them higher and better ways, found his work disturbed and his precepts nullified by the descent of these cruel white fiends upon his community. "Oh father," his poor natives would pray to their ancestors, "defend us from sailing gods who come to steal us in fire-vessels." He spoke of the canoes of native Christians putting forth with courage from the little bay; the unexpected shot discharged at them from the slaver; the surprise of the missionary; the consternation of his flock; the episode of the single sailor who would not let a white man die untended; the nameless horrors of the passage; the natives cooped up in their quarters like pigs or fowls; the total lack of either comfort or decency: then, the approach of the gunboat; the callous cruelty of the skipper and his crew; the vile talk about the "stock"; the sternly practical way in which the order "Chuck them overboard" was given and obeyed. It was a graphic narrative. He had seen with his own eyes, and he made his hearers feel the reality of what he told them. The congregation listened spell-bound. This was not a sermon; it was a genuine piece of native oratory. When he spoke of the thud as each shrieking slave struck the water, with the silence that followed, a hush fell upon his hearers: the whole church was still in an awed access of horror.

But the oddest part of it all was this; as soon as Tom once warmed up to his subject, he forgot where he was; he forgot what he was pretending; he did not even recollect that he must speak in the formal dialect of the pulpit: he remembered only his own burning indignation that such things should be done, and that the flag of his country should be used to cover them. Now and then, indeed, he slipped out unawares some sailor-like colloquialism, for which he forgot to apologise. His hearers smiled; but the earnestness and the *naïveté* of the man and his speech made them not only forgive but actually appreciate these curious little lapses. His sunburnt face, his seafaring manners, his plain English wording, all contributed to his success. Everybody could see—or thought they could see—he was a plain rough missionary, accustomed to the simple life of a Melanesian island, and without graces of manner such as one gets in town churches; but they could also see that he spoke from his very heart, and that the things he described had filled his own soul with the most thrilling horror.

At last he finished with one simple appeal. " Now, what I tell you is no distant fable. These things are being done, to-day, within a fortnight's sail of this port of Sydney. They are being done under cover of the British flag,—the flag that we all love—in order to supply cheap Melanesian labour to British capitalists in a British colony. The people who do them are making that flag hated throughout the South Pacific. Wherever it appears, men fly, and women cower. England is far away: we cannot move her. But I ask you, men and women of Australia, will you help us to rouse her heart and conscience? Will you help us to put down this loathsome blot on our national honour? Will you say at once: ' These things shall not be. The Labour traffic must cease, or must at the very least be civilised and Christianised? ' "

Everybody said it was a most stirring heart-cry. Even capitalists with "interests" in Queensland were moved. " It was not a sermon," Mr. Strong said afterwards, with professional criticism, " but it was an excellent speech, and it carried its audience with it." All Sydney crowded round at the door of St. Jude's to shake hands with the orator. Even Tom himself was dimly aware that day that his fate was now sealed; he could never go back; he had made himself a parson.

When all the others had dropped off, Olive Strong came up. "Thank you, Mr. Glisson," she said. "It was a wonderful description. As you spoke of what you had seen, we all seemed to see it. I knew you could do this thing; and you did it splendidly. I see now quite clearly what your work must be in future. You must stir this matter up in Australia and in England."

Tom was boyishly delighted and pleased with her praise; yet it made him feel more of an impostor and a rogue than ever.

CHAPTER XII.

THE INEVITABLE.

WHEN, long years afterwards, it first began to be privately whispered in England that Cecil Glisson (as everybody called him) was not a clergyman at all, but in forged orders, the few who were inclined to accept that startling rumour took it for granted at once that Cecil Glisson was an unmitigated scoundrel. The crime of personating a priest is one which seems peculiarly heinous to all who accept the inherent sanctity of the clerical calling. Therefore I almost despair of making you understand by what gradual stages, and through what persistent freaks of fate, Tom Pringle fell slowly into this life-long deception. On board the Avenger, he said to himself, it was only till he could reach Sydney. At Sydney, it was only till he could steal away to Melbourne. After that fatal Sunday, it was only still till he could escape from the Strongs. And when once he had fled, Olive Strong must fade away behind him with the rest of this strange phantasmagoric episode in the life of an adventurous Canadian sailor.

That he was a Canadian, too, must be allowed to count for a little in whatever exculpation an apologist may find possible for Tom Pringle's conduct. Not that I am myself concerned to defend or to condemn him; the historian's task is but to state facts as they occur, leaving judgment of good and evil to his readers. Still, it must be admitted in fairness that in European lands the sense of some inherent sanctity in holy orders is stronger by far than in Protestant America, where the man who feels an inner call to preach goes forth and preaches, with or without credentials. And when Tom Pringle grew suddenly conscious that morning at Sydney that he had a message to give to the people of Australia, and that the people would listen to it, he felt himself in some ways more or less justified in the rôle of deception which chance and circumstance had forced upon him.

He lay awake that night none the less, however, and reflected very seriously on his present position. What was he going to do next? For as yet his thoughts were all concentrated on the project of getting free from this awkward fix; he had no idea so far of embarking in a deliberate and life-long deception. He still wanted to steal away to Melbourne or elsewhere; and he had still no design of any other permanent path in life than that of a casual British sailor.

One thing alone stood a little in the way; he would be sorry to say good-bye for ever to Olive.

For Olive was a revelation, an ideal, an epoch. Not since he was a boy in Canada had it happened to him before to speak on equal terms with an English lady. Gently born and bred, he had flung away his ancestral birthright of gentility —the only birthright he had ever possessed— for a boy's love of the sea, a love that rarely lasts much beyond five-and-twenty. And now that he had spent ten days in a house with Olive Strong, he saw his mistake; he began to regret his altered position in society.

Received frankly in that cultivated home as an equal, it suddenly came back to him that he could still be a gentleman. He had had a good many hours alone—when Olive was out—and those hours he had spent for the most part in the library. They suggested to him the idea that after all he did really like books; that he was good for something better, something higher in the world, than reefing sails and lowering jolly-boats. But Olive herself, after all, was the strongest argument. He was aware that if he left Sydney he would leave a great part of himself behind there. As he lay in bed and thought over that distracting day—that day of unexpected and glorious triumph—that day of shameful and incredible deceit—he was most of all conscious that he did not now wish to be a sailor any more, because he was in love with Olive.

And Olive had said one thing, too, that touched him to the core. She talked it all over with him in the drawing-room that evening; and she exclaimed more than once: " That sailor who took you from the canoes and nursed you on the John Wesley must have been a good fellow too. How sad that he should have been blown up in the explosion afterwards! It seems to me he must have been really brave to venture upon having his own way at such a time against that horrid captain."

And Tom could only look down and say: " Oh, yes, he was a good fellow enough; " which under the circumstances seemed painfully lukewarm. This odd conflict of real modesty with the curious fear of seeming to underrate the man who, according to the official story, had saved his life, was difficult to carry off with a becoming demeanour. Before he quite knew what was happening he found himself engaged in a glowing eulogy of his own tenderness as a nurse and a touching tribute to his own dead memory.

In the small hours of the night, he half laughed to himself at the absurdity of the situation. It would have been immensely comic, if it were not so embarrassing. But he felt none the less that the affair was growing a trifle too complicated. Sooner or later, he must go. And the sooner the better.

Filled with this idea, he rose early next morning, determined, like a foolish young sailor that he was, on a somewhat precipitate line of action. It was no use loitering. He must break away at once. He must get rid for ever of these lying black clothes; he must return to the sea and be an honest sailor.

Determined to act, he dressed himself in Cecil Glisson's red cross shirt, and descended to the drawing-room. A fever of penitence was on him—the first of many from which he suffered during a life of alternate emotions, all fiercely suppressed under a calm exterior. He had behaved abominably; he could feel that now; yet he had taken the only possible alternative that he could see to being unjustly hanged for participation in acts which horrified and revolted him. Nay, would it not even have been wrong in him to let such a travesty of justice take its course without an effort to prevent it? And how else could he prevent it save in the way he had chosen?

Yet he was really penitent. Above all, for his attitude towards that innocent Olive. He had unwillingly and almost unwittingly deceived her; but he had deceived her for all that; and he respected her so much that the sense of having deceived her was odious and unendurable to his candid nature.

So now he had made up his mind to steal away without even saying good-bye to her; to embark on a ship for some distant port; and then to write in general and non-committing terms about the gross deception he had practised upon her.

If so, how could he sign it? Cecil Glisson? To do that would be to put a hateful slight upon the memory of the man whom he had nursed and admired and wronged and personated. Tom Pringle? To do that would be to play once more into the hands of injustice and secure his own hanging; for Tom knew that in these days the police of the world, like a banded brotherhood, can track a suspected criminal from Sydney to San Francisco and from Temuka to Constantinople, Rio, or Petersburg. This, however, was a remoter difficulty, which he was not now called upon for the moment to solve; though it occurred to him even then that if he fled away suddenly, he might suggest the notion that he was not Cecil Glisson; and if that notion were once suggested, and enquiry aroused, it would go hard under the circumstances if they did not hang him. For if, when he first landed, he had proclaimed himself as Tom Pringle, and told the whole truth, it was just conceivable, though scarcely probable, that people might have believed him; but now that he had played the part of the missionary successfully for ten days together, and even preached with unction an affecting sermon, all the world would conclude he was one of the pirate gang, unless he was Glisson; and hanged he would be more certainly than ever.

Yet he was prepared to risk that last terrible chance itself rather than continue any longer his gross deception of the girl he was beginning to confess himself in love with.

It was early morning, and he had crept down furtively into the dining-room. He was on the prowl after food, for even in such desperate straits, a man must feed; and he had just succeeded in finding a loaf of bread in the sideboard, when steps on the stairs aroused him. He paused and listened. It was a woman's tread. He listened again and felt sure it was Olive descending. Now, Tom was quite prepared to face mere hanging, but he was not prepared to face such a ridiculous position as being caught by that angel in the act of stealing a loaf of bread from her sideboard. He beat a hasty retreat, and, finding no other way open, retired on to the verandah. Then, terrified lest Olive should look out and see him, he crouched for a while behind a long wicker chair, and waited to fly till Olive should disappear again.

He heard her open the dining-room door and peer in. He heard her approach the window. He had left it unfastened, of course. She looked out, glanced around, and surveyed the garden. At the same moment, he heard the study door open. He knew that Mr. Strong used to rise very early to write his sermons, but he had hardly expected him quite as early as this. A voice called out: " Olive! "

" Yes, Papa."

" What are you doing, up at this hour? "

Mr. Strong had come into the dining-room by this time, and Olive had left the window open. Tom, crouched behind his wicker chair, could hear every word they spoke as easily as if he had been in the room with them. Olive's tone had something of hesitation in it as she answered uneasily: " I thought I heard Mr. Glisson come down, and I was afraid he might be ill or in want of something; so I slipped on my dress and just ran down to ask him."

" Olive, you are thinking too much of this Mr. Glisson."

" Am I, Papa? " He could feel her heart beating in the voice with which she said it.

" Yes, my child, you are. I have seen it for some days. I have watched till I was sure. And. I'm doubly sorry for it. In the first place, he means nothing; he's too full of his work, and too eager to get back again, to think of anything else. And in the second place, you know very well, you don't want to go to Temuka."

Olive paused a second. Then she answered slowly. " That's quite true in one way; I don't want to go to Temuka. But I could go anywhere, Papa, with—a man that loved me."

Mr. Strong drew an audible breath. " It's as bad as that, then, is it? " he asked. " You've been thinking it over, and you'd be prepared to go, even to Temuka? "

" How do I know, Papa? " Olive answered demurely. " Nobody has asked me yet. If I were asked—by somebody—I would take time, I suppose, to consider my answer."

She said it as lightly as she could; but Tom

was aware where he lurked that she said it with a restrained air which meant a great deal. She was trying to laugh it off because it meant so much to her.

" Olive, you're in love with this young man."

She dropped her voice.

" I—I suppose so."

" And he has nothing to marry upon."

" That doesn't matter. He has courage, and cleverness, and a great deal beside. Everyone said on Sunday they never heard such a sermon."

" Ah, that was because he was describing what he had seen and gone through. He forgot himself wholly in his dramatic story. I don't know whether he could preach at all on any ordinary subject."

" I don't know either. He can do better than that. He can make one listen when he talks about what he knows. And as to going to Temuka, why should he ever go back again? He has better work to do here, a thousand times better, and you ought to tell him so. He would be of infinitely more use in New South Wales than thrown away on a Melanesian island."

" Olive, take care! you overrate his abilities."

" No I don't, Papa. He's far cleverer than he knows; only, he's much too modest. He could do anything that he tried. I can hear by all he tells us how extremely clever he is, if only he had some one to spur him on, and if he lived where he could make any use of his cleverness."

"I ought never to have asked him here," Mr. Strong broke out. "I might have foreseen, of course, that this would happen. But as local secretary of the Society, I thought I must ask him; and he's a nice young fellow too, and I confess, I took a fancy to him."

"So did I," Olive answered simply.

Her father laughed. Poor Tom, behind the chair, felt guiltier than ever. His face was fiery red; he could feel it burning. He hardly knew what to do. Oh, suppose they were only to find him hiding there!

"Well, where is he?" the father asked.

"I don't know," Olive answered. "He *must* have come down, because his bedroom door's open; and besides, he has unfastened this window; you shut it yourself last night, you know, and none of the servants are down yet. I'm afraid he's ill, or else he's gone out in the garden."

The father went off to search the grounds for the truant. Olive turned into the drawing-room. The moment she was gone, Tom felt it was now or never. He must bolt for the front gate and be done for ever with this impossible situation. He crept noiselessly to the steps, and made a dart for the gate. As he did so, Olive stepped out once more on to the verandah. Tom stood facing her for a second, in his red cross shirt, with his face somewhat redder. Then, overcome by shame, he sank into the long wicker chair, covered his face with his hands, and half laughed, half cried, half groaned, half sobbed in his perplexity and confusion.

CHAPTER XIII.

VITA NUOVA.

OLIVE'S face, too, was crimson, for she dimly felt the young man had heard all. She looked down at him with her steady eyes, now troubled for a second. "Where were you going, Mr. Glisson?" she asked very tremulously.

Tom told the truth for once, and shamed the devil. "I—I was going away, Miss Strong," he answered slowly. "Stealing away, unperceived, like a thief in the night. I ought never to have come. And I was trying to undo the first false step—by taking a second."

He could face her like a man, now, for he was no longer dressed up in those ridiculous canonicals.

Olive gazed at him, irresolute. Her face was flushed; her cheeks were burning. "I don't understand you," she cried, grasping a chair for support, and feeling the world reel round her. "You—were going to leave us?"

Tom leant over her, in an agony, torn asunder

between despair and love. " I was going to leave you," he repeated resolutely. " It was the only way out. I have put myself in a false position: I was trying to escape from it. I did wrong to come at all. And—your father does not want me."

" You heard us? " Olive gasped, with a wild flush of shame.

Tom put the devil to the blush again. " Yes, unintentionally, unwillingly, I heard you. I was trying to slink away from the house unperceived, when you came down hurriedly. I stepped out here on the verandah, and did my best to hide. I could not foresee what was going to happen. Then your father called; and—Miss Strong, Miss Strong—forgive me, believe me—I really *couldn't* help it."

Olive stood glued to the spot. Her face was on fire now. Her heart stood still. Her breath came and went with difficulty. She could only repeat in a dazed and terrified undertone: " You heard us! *You* heard us! "

Tom seized her hand in his. There was nothing else left to do. " Yes, Miss Strong," he cried; " Olive—I have surprised your secret. But you have surprised mine too. What *you* feel, *I* feel. I did not mean to tell you. I knew I had no right. I had thought every word of what your father said, before he said it. It would be wrong of me to ask such a woman as you to link your life with mine. I knew it; I recognised it. And yet, . . . every day that I spent in this house, I admired and longed for you more each minute." He leaned eagerly forward. " I loved you, Olive. And *because* I loved you, and *because* I knew I could never ask you to be my wife, I was trying to steal away—when you came down and prevented me. What else could I do? Ask your own heart that. If I stayed, I must fall deeper and deeper in love with you. And I knew from the very first my love was quite hopeless."

Olive looked up at him through the tears that began to fill her eyes. "*Why*, Mr. Glisson? " she asked slowly.

The delicious simplicity and unexpectedness of that answer took Tom's breath away with a tremor of delight and happiness. So Olive wanted him! His voice had the clear ring of truth in it; and Olive had recognised it at once. She saw this man loved her; and *if* he loved her, what else could matter? She knew that in these matters there is no such word as impossible. And when she asked " Why, Mr. Glisson? " Tom's heart gave one wild bound. It would have bounded harder if she had said " Why,

Mr. Pringle?" The sense of that continued deception alone prevented him from rising to the seventh heavens.

He grasped her hand tighter. "Because—" he answered, scarcely knowing what he said, and casting about him for some adequate reason, "I am quite a poor man, with nothing to depend upon but my very small salary." (What was Glisson's salary, he wondered, and who the dickens paid it?) "Because—I could never dream of taking you to Temuka. Because—your father would not give his consent. Because— it would be mean to repay his hospitality so ill. Because—it would be wrong of me to tie a life like yours to my own poor fortunes."

"And—you were really going to leave me?" Olive repeated, clinging to his hand with a sense of terror as if she thought he would withdraw it—which, to do Tom justice, was far at that moment from his intention. "To leave me without one word, without a good-bye, even!"

Tom had an irresistible impulse. Parson or no parson, impostor or honest man, he was only aware at that instant that a woman who loved him was clinging to his hand; and with a great flood of feeling, he stooped down and kissed her. He did it with reverence, with reluctance almost;

he was profoundly aware as his lips touched hers how unworthy he was of that pure, calm woman. Even if he had not been playing a part, a mean, deceptive part, he would have felt it more than a little; for Tom had that kind of chivalry which recognises at once its own infinite inferiority to a good woman's heart. But as things stood, he hated himself for the desecration he was committing. To be perfectly frank, Tom, who was no ecclesiast, felt much more acutely the desecration of which he was guilty by that kiss to Olive than he had felt the desecration of mounting the pulpit steps as an ordained priest on Sunday morning. The one was a thing that he could fully understand; it came within his purview: the other belonged to a special range of thought, as yet unfamiliar to him. He had still to learn it, in sackcloth and ashes.

Still, he stooped down and kissed her. And unworthy as he knew himself to touch those pure lips, he was yet aware as he did so of a strange inrush of feeling, a sort of ineffable wave from heaven. He lingered on them for a second. As for Olive, she took the kiss with a sense as of her right. She loved him; he loved her; that was all she thought about.

Her hand tightened on his. The blush died away from her face. If *he* felt like that, she had no cause to be ashamed. Their secret was mutual. She looked up into his face and murmured gently: " Then, you love me—Cecil? "

" Cecil! " That " Cecil " brought Tom back with a horrid thud to solid earth again. The seventh heavens melted away. A pang darted through his heart. More than ever before, he knew the die was cast now. There was no going back from this. He had sealed his fate, and bound himself in honour for life to Olive.

Yet, what a horrible outlook! Must he go on for years with this odious deception? Must he begin love's dream under false pretences? Must he marry the woman he loved under another man's name? Must he shuffle off himself and pass his life henceforth with somebody else's personality. The thought was hateful to him. Had he had time to reflect, he would probably have decided that such a course was too dangerous. Apart even from its wickedness, he would have doubted his own ability to sustain for long years so difficult a deception. But it was Tom Pringle's misfortune that he had *never* time to reflect, to deliberate, to resolve, at any one of these great crises. Events forced him to act at once; and, acting at once on the spur of the moment, without any fixed intention of embarking on a career of crime, he yet found himself led step by step, half against his will, into abysses unfathomable.

So now, a man's virile instinct compelled him to refrain from serious thought, and to lean down and murmur: " Why, Olive, I loved you from the moment I first saw you, here on the verandah."

Her fingers tightened on his hand again, and she gave a little satisfied gasp. If he really loved her—if she had not forced him into an unwilling avowal—she cared for nothing else. He might see into her heart—if only his was hers already.

" And yet," she whispered, half chiding, " you were going to run away from me! "

He gave a despairing gesture. " Olive, what else could I do? What else can I do now? I have no right to make love to you. What will your father say? He will think I have taken a dishonourable advantage of his hospitable kindness. He will say I should never have ventured to dream of you."

Olive looked deep into his eyes again. " I wouldn't mind *that*," she answered. " This is a question for *me*. I love Papa dearly—he is the kindest and best of fathers. But a girl's heart is her own. Her own, not her father's."

" To you and me, yes. But fathers do not think so."

"He will think so soon. Cecil, I have no fear for you. I know you are cleverer and greater than you think. That is one of the very things that makes me love you. I see you are so modest about your own abilities. But—where did you mean to go? What were you going to do with yourself? If you ran away from Papa like that, you could never have gone back as a missionary to Temuka."

"Olive, I will tell you the truth. I was going back—to be a common sailor."

With a mighty effort he had braced himself up for it. He meant to confess all. And if only Olive had understood his meaning, he would really have confessed it. But the same moral ill luck pursued him throughout. Olive did not notice the ambiguous phrase " going back." She fastened only on the last words of his sentence. "To be a common sailor!" she cried. "How do you mean? You would have given up the church, and gone to sea for always?"

The horror in her voice at the bare idea checked him. He answered evasively, with a hang-dog air: "What else was open to me? I couldn't have returned to Temuka, if I slank away like a thief from your father's house; and I couldn't tell your father I meant to leave because I had fallen in love with his daughter and knew myself utterly unworthy to ask her." The psychological moment had passed, and he had not taken advantage of it.

"And for my sake, you would have given up everything, and begun life over again?"

Tom reflected to himself that he had not much to give up—a common sailor's off-chance: and this false ascription of heroism was hateful to his real nature. But what could he say? He had not strength of mind to confess the whole truth when it came to the push—especially as to confess would be to make Olive hate him. He could only murmur: "I could begin life over again easily enough, for I should only be giving up a savage hut in a wild island. And a sailor's place can hardly be much worse than a missionary's in Melanesia."

"But I mean you to be something much more than that," Olive cried, with a girl's confidence in her chosen lover, her eyes growing prouder. "I mean you to do work that all the world will praise and admire. You are mine now, and it is my place to inspire you. *I* know what you are worth, and *you* do not. For that, I love you. But I am going to take care that you realise your own value. You shall never be thrown away on a Pacific Island."

Tom looked at her admiringly. With a

woman like this to spur one on to great things, a man might surely rise to be anything. He had no exalted opinion of his own abilities—indeed, Olive was right; he was much too modest: but he knew he had a good memory and a taste for languages; and as to intelligence, why, hang it all——

Mem., that if he was really going to be a parson henceforth, he must dismiss for the future this tell-tale sailor habit of saying " hang it all," or worse, at every turn of the conversation.

Well, hang it all, then, or don't hang it; he had surprised himself the other day by the ease with which he read Cecil Glisson's Greek Testament. Perhaps he had more brains than he had ever suspected.

He gazed back at Olive with unaffected delight. " Do you really think," he said, " I might be good for something—in Australia, for instance? "

Olive gazed back at him with a girl's proud trust in the man who has won her. " I think," she answered with the ring of conviction, " you could do anything you liked. And now you are mine, I mean to make you do it."

Even as she said it, a voice came from behind the big wattle-bush on the edge of the lawn. " I've searched for him everywhere, Olive, and

I can't find him, up or down. He's not in the garden, I'm certain."

"No, Papa," Olive answered, growing suddenly hot again. "He's here on the verandah, —and I am with him."

CHAPTER XIV.

CROSSING THE RUBICON.

THERE was something in her tone which told her father that much had happened while he went round the garden. He moved up the steps hurriedly. Olive had dropped Tom's hand, and stood opposite him now with a sweet new expression lighting up her face; her eyes were downcast, but she did not attempt otherwise to conceal her feelings. Tom had a guilty look upon his countenance, but was nevertheless as mitigatedly happy as a man can be who has won a good girl's love by a regrettable subterfuge. The father took it all in at once. To say the truth, it needed no Columbus to make that discovery. " Well," he murmured slowly. " You have found him? "

" Yes," Olive answered with meaning, lifting her calm eyes to his face. " We have found one another."

There was a long pause. Then Mr. Strong remarked curtly: " So I see." Nobody said much else. But all three understood one another.

Olive stood for a minute, undecided. After a very short pause, she took Tom's hand in hers. "Good-bye for the present," she said, letting it drop. And she glided upstairs again.

Tom was left, flushed and trembling, face to face with the hostile element of a father.

Again there was a pause. Mr. Strong waited for Tom to begin. Tom waited for Mr. Strong. Neither felt quite easy. At last, a faint smile played round the clergyman's lips. He knew Olive well, and he knew therefore that if Olive had made up her mind, a father was, after all, a mere spectator, called in at the last moment to ratify her decisions. "Well?" he observed once more, interrogatively.

Tom sank into a chair, a picture of perplexity.

"What do you propose to do next?" the elder man asked with emphasis.

Thus driven to bay, Tom rushed into it at once. "I don't know," he answered. "That's just what puzzles me. It has all come upon me so suddenly. I didn't guess it myself at all till just now. That is to say," he corrected, "I didn't mean to confess it. But—but circumstances were too strong for me. An Occasion arose three minutes since—and the Occasion was inevitable.

It wasn't really my fault. Set it down to coincidence."

He stammered and stumbled. Mr. Strong more than half understood the situation—so far as Olive was concerned, at least; for he knew already she was in love with the new comer. "And you have arrived at an understanding?" he put in tentatively at last.

"Oh, dear me, no!" Tom exclaimed. "I would not venture to presume. We—we just read one another's eyes, that's all—little more. An understanding—far from it. But,—in a way, I think Miss Strong—well, no, not that: I don't know how to put it. Nothing at all has passed; still, perhaps, she infers from what I said to her just now that I—admire her greatly."

"I see," the father answered with chilly reserve.

Tom threw himself at once on the elder man's mercy. "But I didn't mean to speak," he cried. "I assure you I didn't mean it. You must really forgive me. I know how unjustifiable it was; how wrong; how foolish. I have nothing to offer her; absolutely nothing: and I would not have dared to offer it—did not offer it in fact—only —well, I think I had better explain exactly. I felt I was falling in love, and I felt it was wrong of me, and I didn't want to repay your hospitality so ill; so—I got up this morning meaning to slink away from Sydney, and then to write to you explaining my reasons; because I was too nervous to say to your face that—" He broke down utterly. " Oh, Mr. Strong," he cried, trembling, and leaning eagerly forward, with his brown hands clasped, " you must make some allowances for me. I am a rough man from the sea, and I'm not used now to the ways of civilisation. And a lady is strange to me—so strange, so novel, so wonderful, so to be worshipped. The mere touch of her hand thrilled me. It wasn't my fault if I fell in love at sight; and having fallen in love, what could I do as a man of honour but run away at once when I knew it was impossible? "

" You are not quite articulate," the father said, smiling grimly.

" I know it," Tom answered. " I am quite inarticulate. I am no great speaker. And that was one reason why I felt it was absurd, impossible for me to dream of her. I would not have dreamt of her. I refrained from dreaming of her. I tried to leave her. But if I find *she* dreams of of *me*—Mr. Strong, I am a man; and we are most of us human! "

" Do I understand," the father asked, half

annoyed, half amused, at his evident earnestness, "that you really contemplated running away from this house without so much as even saying good-bye to us?"

Tom gave a gesture of deprecation. "I was driven to it," he answered.

"And do you think that is conduct of a sort to encourage a father in entrusting you for life with his daughter's happiness?"

"No, I don't," Tom blurted out doggedly. "If you want the plain truth, I think I was a fool; but I think I was hard put to it; and when a man's a fool, and is also hard put to it,—I ask you as a man, is it kind to make him feel his position too acutely?"

Mr. Strong sat down and gazed at him. "Now, this is serious," he said slowly. "You have told me nothing; but you have told me enough to see that it is serious. Am I to understand that you consider yourself engaged to my daughter Olive?"

"I'm sure I don't know," Tom cried. "I have said hardly anything to her. It wasn't what we *said;* it was—the way we looked at one another."

"And does Olive consider herself engaged to you?"

"I can't tell you," Tom cried, growing more

and more helpless. Then a happy thought struck him. "You had better ask her."

Mr. Strong gave him a respite of five minutes while he went upstairs. Now was a chance for Tom to get away if he wanted. Half an hour ago he would have seized it. The half hour between had completely altered the face of life for him. There was no more going back. He realised now that he was bound to Olive; which implied that henceforth he was Cecil Glisson.

He sat there, deeply in love, as happy as a king, and supremely miserable.

"Olive," the father asked, when after a short delay she opened her door to him, "I want to ask, is this young man engaged to you?"

Olive's eyes were wet with happy tears. She met her father's gaze fearlessly. "I don't know whether he's *engaged* to me," she answered; "he said nothing about engagement; but *I'm* engaged to him; I am his, for ever."

She said it so simply, so strongly, so resolutely, that her father, who knew her, accepted her word as irrevocable. "Very well," he said in a slow voice; "if that is so, what do you propose he should do for the future?"

Olive reflected a second. "It's all so new," she answered; "so fresh; so undecided. It broke upon us so suddenly. We haven't any plans.

We have said nothing to one another, asked each other no questions. I only know I love him, and I'm sure he loves me. We have neither of us gone beyond that stage for the present."

"Doesn't that seem to you unwise?" her father asked with the voice of parental prudence.

"We mustn't be precipitate," Olive answered with the wisdom of youth. "We haven't thought about these things yet. But of one thing I am sure. Cecil will not go back any more to Temuka."

"Are you certain of that? He seemed so set upon it."

"Yes; that was before. And it didn't really mean that he wanted himself to go back to Temuka; it meant, he was afraid to stop here any longer; because he knew beforehand in his heart what was coming."

"This is very foolish, Olive. You are engaging yourself to a man without a chance of marrying."

"It *would* be foolish, with some men. But not with him. I feel quite sure of him. He is better than rich. If he has nothing, that will only be a spur to exertion."

An hour later, in the drawing-room, Olive told Tom so, plainly. She was not in the least shy of him now. Perfect love casteth out fear;

and she was far too much in love to think of anything else save what she needed to tell him.

"Do you think I can ever do anything?" Tom asked once more.

"I'm sure of it," Olive answered with an overflowing confidence that inspired him in turn. "You would have done great things already if you hadn't been wasted on a Pacific Island. You have been set to teach savages when you were fit for much higher work. What you have to do now is to begin a crusade—here, at once, in New South Wales—against this traffic that you hate and that almost killed you. You mustn't go back to Temuka—Papa can arrange all that. He pulls the wires of the Society. You must stop here and organise. You will be serving the mission far better so than by returning to the Islands. And Papa can settle with the Society at home "—"at home" meaning England—"that you shall be engaged upon this work instead of the other."

"But—am I fit for work in Australia?" Tom asked. "Remember, I am only a wild man of the sea. I have never laid myself out for a civilised congregation."

"Then what you have to do now is to lay yourself out for it. You can do that if you try; you must know it yourself as well as I know it.

You can fit yourself for anything. It is only your modesty that prevents you from seeing it."

Tom gave a slight sigh. "But it will be years," he said, "such years, before I can ever hope—"

Olive waved her capable hand. "What does that matter? I can wait years for you if necessary. But it will not be necessary. You will be asked to take some big church soon; I feel quite certain of it."

Her very voice inspired him with unwonted confidence. He began to think better of himself than ever before. If Tom Pringle was loyal to anything in his future life, he was loyal to Olive. He admired, respected, and loved her intensely; he had reason to love her; for it was she who had made him. But when the terrible doubt came at last, and he saw his own act in ecclesiastical colours, he used often to console himself with the thought that it was not altogether his own fault that he had become a false clergyman; it was Olive who did it, unwittingly, innocently. Olive had made up her mind that he was to advance in the Church, not for filthy lucre's sake, but because she believed in him; because she loved him; she was sure he could do great things, and therefore she made him do them. "Surely," he thought to himself often,

" some allowance will be made, when my life is judged, for the magnitude of the temptation, for the concatenation of events, for the inevitableness of my action." He did it all, he knew, not wholly for mere love of Olive, but partly for love, and partly because he saw no other way out of an impossible situation.

However, since Olive had decided that a clergyman he was to be, and a town clergyman at that, he must honestly set to work to prepare for his vocation. He must fit himself for his position. And Tom Pringle's habit was to do with his heart whatever he undertook. So that very morning saw him seated at a table in Mr. Strong's study, with Cecil Glisson's Greek Testament spread out before him, flanked by Pearson on the Creed, Liddell and Scott's Lexicon, and a large blank note-book. As yet, to be sure, Tom had no views of his own on the nature of holy orders; or to be more strictly accurate his views were a sailor's; but he had a certain honest dogged British determination that if he were really Cecil Glisson, and a parson to boot, he must do his work like a man, and prove himself a labourer worthy of his hire.

You will think, no doubt, the two points of view inconsistent. But that is possibly because you are not an able-bodied mariner.

CHAPTER XV.

THE PALACE, DORCHESTER.

THE Bishop of Dorchester sat at his dinner table with Sir Edward Colbeck. It was a cool June evening, after a clear westerly-blowing day, and countless throats of nightingales were discoursing vespers in the grounds of the Palace. The Bishop had a dignified, clean-cut face, with a philanthropic expression that was not entirely professional. Mrs. Glisson sat opposite him, calm, sedate, matronly, her beautiful smooth hair just beginning to be touched with no unkindly hand of time by the gentle grey of comely middle age. Evelyn faced Sir Edward. It was a family party.

Dorchester Palace is not, as many ill-informed people suppose, in Dorsetshire. The house stands in a bight of the chalk downs on the banks of the Thames, near the Oxfordshire town of the same name; its beautiful grounds slope down

137

to the water's edge with a smooth declivity of green English turf, broken here and there by tall flowering clumps of rhododendron and azalea. It has no wide view, indeed, but makes up for it by what the eighteenth century would have described as a *prospect*—a pretty glimpse over a lawn, past a spreading copper beech and some noble cedars, to a blue reach of the river.

The Palace itself, though comparatively new, has been quickly draped over by fast-growing creepers. A huge wistaria hangs its pendent blue clusters in a cataract of bloom along the river front;. a large-leaved aristolochia mantles the posts of the verandah with its pale green foliage; banksia roses and honeysuckle fall in a riot of blossom over the upper floors; Virginia creeper droops in waving sprays from the finials of the gable end. The grey stone of the wall and the jutting corbels show just enough in between to make the architecture of the present day pass muster at a hasty glance for that of the fifteenth century. Seen from the Thames, indeed, Dorchester Palace ranks, says the local guide book, as the most picturesque house between Windsor and Oxford. The dining-room looks out in one direction on the Thames, while it commands on the other a delicious glimpse of the mouldering old minster.

" Yes," Sir Edward remarked, helping himself to another olive; " it was lucky you put in that postscript about your county. When I saw your address at the head of your note-paper, ' Dorchester Palace, Oxfordshire,' I didn't pay any particular attention to the last word; and, knowing but one Dorchester, in Dorset, I naturally would have run down there, if you hadn't warned me that this was another place of the same name."

" Most people make that mistake," Evelyn put in. " I always tell Papa he ought to add in italics on the die, ' *not* Dorset '; but he thinks that would be *infra dig.* I hate *dig.* for my part. He says everybody ought to know the dioceses of England."

" Well, *I* didn't, anyhow," Sir Edward answered frankly. He was a portly and thick-set Philistine, of the self-complacent moneyed order. " Never heard till to-day there was more than one Dorchester. *And* with a cathedral, too; a real old cathedral; not one of these new-fangled modern things like Truro, but a mediæval minster! "

" It was not a cathedral in the middle ages," the Bishop put in anxiously:—" at least, I mean, not the existing building. The building you now see was only a monastery church of the Augustinian abbey. It's mostly thirteenth century, and we've just restored it. But earlier still, of course, this Oxfordshire Dorchester was a place of great importance. It ranks as one of our earliest English cathedral towns. In a certain sense,"—the Bishop poised his two hands before him with the finger-tips meeting—" I may be said to occupy the chair of Birinus."

He said it with the conscious air of a man who imparts to his hearer a striking piece of information.

" Oh, indeed? " Sir Edward murmured, pouring out a second glass of port. " That's *very* interesting." The native curiosity overcame him. " Though, now I come to think of it," he went on, eying the port with the light through it, " who or what was Birinus? "

Evelyn looked up at him mischievously. " Oh, Sir Edward," she said, " you don't know what you've let yourself in for. When once Papa gets started upon the subject of Birinus, we know that the history of Dorchester in six volumes is bound to follow, with digressions on the dioceses of Winchester and Lincoln, and the various sees into which they have been divided. When you said, ' That's *very* interesting,' in such a voice of conviction, Papa thought you knew all about Birinus already, and was going to let you off. Now you fly straight into it, as Big-wood says about the partridges when Mr. Watson shoots, and you'll have the whole subject in the regulation six volumes."

Mrs. Glisson looked across at her daughter with gentle reproof in her eyes. "Evelyn dear," she said softly, "Papa knows so much more than anybody else about the history of the church that visitors are naturally glad to hear all about it from him."

"Besides," Sir Edward interposed, "now the question has been raised, I really want to know about this fellow Birinus who made the chair the Bishop is sitting in. I'm fond of old furniture. I suppose he was some mediæval Chippendale or Sheraton."

The Bishop coughed slightly. "When I said I sat in the seat of Birinus," he answered, looking sideways with a repressive glance at Evelyn, who was disposed to laugh, "I employed a metaphor: I did not mean it literally but figuratively. Birinus, in point of fact, was the first bishop of Dorchester; or, to be more strictly accurate, the first bishop *in* Dorchester; for bishoprics at that time were tribal rather than local; there was a Bishop of the West Saxons, not a Bishop of Wessex nor a Bishop of Winchester; there was a Bishop of the Kentings, not a Bishop of Kent nor a Bishop of Canterbury; there was a Bishop of the Mercians, not a Bishop of Mercia nor a Bishop of Lichfield. In the Anglo-Saxon language "—Evelyn made a wry face—" a bishopric is oftenest described as a bishop-stool—a literal translation, of course, of *see*, the Latin *sedes*. So when I say that I sit in the chair of Birinus, I mean merely to convey that I occupy in a sense the pastoral direction of the same diocese, or part of it."

"Ah, I see," Sir Edward answered, glancing sympathetically at Evelyn. He began to perceive the nature of her objection to starting the Bishop on mediæval history.

But the Bishop was started now, and was not to be easily stopped. " Dorchester," he continued, putting the forefingers and thumbs of both hands together once more in a sort of leaf-shape above his finger-glass, " Dorchester, you will recollect, was the original capital of the West-Saxon kings; this Oxfordshire Dorchester, Dorchester-on-Thames, not in Oxfordshire then, for neither Oxford nor counties as yet existed. It was the royal city of Cynegils,"—" I beg your pardon," Sir Edward ejaculated. " Cynegils," the Bishop repeated blandly,—" the first Christion king of the West-Saxons. In 635, you must be aware, the Pope sent Birinus, a North Italian monk, to convert the West-Saxons, about forty years after St. Augustine of Canterbury had converted the Kentishmen. Now, Cynegils had his court here at Dorchester; so to Dorchester accordingly Birinus came; and unless I mistake, he baptised the English king over yonder in the Thames, at a spot close to that large clump of rhododendrons which we planted last autumn. Baptism by immersion was then still universal; Baeda—the Venerable Bede, as people call him nowadays—mentions no other method."

"We planted *white* rhododendrons," Mrs. Glisson interposed, " as a memento of the fact— white being of course the symbolical colour of baptismal regeneration."

" There's such a funny little picture of the baptism of this king with the dreadful name," Evelyn put in once more, " in an illuminated missal Papa has upstairs in his library. It shows the old gentleman and his nobles all undressing on the bank—with the ladies as well—and such a funny little bishop, in a mitre and a dalmatic or whatever you call it, standing on the river shore with two fingers up, like this, blessing them. It *is* so comical."

" And that illumination," the Bishop added, " has fortunately enabled me to identify the precise spot pointed out by tradition as being the scene of the admission of the people of Wessex into the Christian church. It was drawn from nature by an Augustinian monk of this very abbey about 1430, and it clearly points to the bank just below the clump of white rhododendrons as being the actual place where Birinus administered the sacrament of baptism. It is a very precious document." (If the Bishop *had* a fault, it was a faint deficiency in the sense of humour.)

"Dear me!" Sir Edward murmured, beginning to yawn. "How very interesting!"

When a man says "How very interesting!" twice over in the same conversation, wise people know that the subject bores him, and (unless they are prigs) they proceed at once to another. But the Bishop still retained too much of Tom Pringle's pristine innocence ever to recognise that a subject which interested *him* might bore other people. So he merely answered: "Yes, it *is* very interesting. One feels that here one has got down, so to speak, to the very bed-rock of British Christianity. At Dorchester, we touch bottom. There, in this self-same Thames, which has gone on flowing unceasingly from that day to this, by yonder tussock of sedge, the Latin monk from Lombardy, dispatched by Pope Honorius, baptised in running water after the older form the heathen king of the West-Saxons, and so founded the bishopric which I now—unworthily—occupy. Is it not a strange thought that I here, to-day, am the representative of Birinus in the seventh century?"

"I don't think anybody else feels this continuity of history quite so vividly as my husband," Mrs. Glisson added with a look of deep wifely admiration.

"It is you who have made me feel it, dear," the Bishop replied, returning her look with interest. "Not, of course, that the continuity is here quite unbroken. I said that, in a sense, I occupy to-day the bishop-stool of Birinus. But it is only in a sense; I admit that unreservedly. In one way—the truest way, my excellent colleague, the Bishop of Winchester, represents the original see of the West-Saxon kingdom; which is why, of course, the Bishop of Winchester ranks first after the Primates among English bishops."

"Indeed," Sir Edward interjected. He was a Member of Parliament from an industrial Lancashire borough, and history began for him with the invention of the cotton jenny.

"Yes," the unconscious Bishop continued, toying aimlessly with his wineglass. "The descent, I must admit, is indirect. Birinus, who baptised Cynegils over yonder by the rhododendrons—St. Oswald of Northumbria, you know, was his sponsor—Birinus was Bishop of the West-Saxons; and the West-Saxons at that early age held the whole Thames valley. Their kingdom extended as far as the Severn. But later, Wulfhere of Mercia drove them across the Thames, and annexed all what was afterwards known as Oxfordshire. Owing to that conquest, the West-Saxon kings retired to Winchester, which became thenceforth their capital. Indeed, when the kings of Wessex grew into kings of England in the person of Edgar—*not* as is usually but incorrectly stated of Egbert—" at this point the Bishop made a rhetorical pause so as to lay especial stress on his own pet hobby—" Winchester was really the capital of the whole country."

" Is that so? " Sir Edward exclaimed, not knowing exactly what remark was expected of him, and fingering the heavy gold seal on his heavy gold watch-chain. The chain and the waistcoat that formed its background were the salient points of Sir Edward's physiognomy.

" Oh, yes," the Bishop answered, warming up to his subject; " Winchester was the capital of England, not only under Alfred, but even under William the Conqueror. It was but slowly superseded by London, or rather by Westminster, owing to the importance of Edward the Confessor's minster. In that sense, then, that he is still the representative West-Saxon Bishop, my dear friend at Winchester is the successor of Birinus. Then again, Dorchester was afterwards the seat of the Mercian bishops from Wulfhere's conquest till 1073—or was it 1074?—I forget the exact date, but at any rate, some time in William the Conqueror's reign; when Remigius removed the see to Lincoln. In that sense, therefore, Dr. Blenkinsopp is really the successor of Birinus, or at any rate of the historical bishopric of Dorchester."

"I see," Sir Edward answered with a mute look of appeal to Evelyn. But Evelyn only smiled a familiar little smile and expanded her hands as who should say, "You *would* rush into it. If you get it all now, you've only yourself to blame. Don't say I didn't warn you."

"I need hardly add," the Bishop went on, "that not one stone of the existing cathedral dates back to the days when Dorchester was still an old Saxon bishopric. The minster which Remigius deserted for the Roman hill of Lincoln was no doubt a wooden one. But the site had always ecclesiastical importance; and in the later middle ages, when the Thames became the main highway of Plantagenet England, the Augustinian monks built the beautiful church over which I am now permitted to preside—" he uttered that word "permitted" with a touch of something more than conventional episcopal modesty;—"the greater part of it being of the thirteenth century, as you can see for yourself by glancing out of this window."

Sir Edward rose and looked at it casually. He could see nothing of the sort; for his knowledge of architecture was a negative quantity; but he contented himself with saying in a tone of cheap conviction: "Dear me, you don't say so."

"And when the crying need for an increase in the episcopate began to be deeply felt," the Bishop went on, quite unconscious of his hearer's boredom, "it was natural that a site so long connected with the Church in one form or another, and possessing so splendid an old historical building, should be chosen as the seat of one of the new dioceses. I urged it myself; I advocated the division of the diocese from the beginning; I always said, long before it occurred to me that anybody could consider me worthy to occupy a place on the episcopal bench, 'Dorchester is the proper seat for the new bishop.'"

"Oh, but he did much more than that, Sir Edward," Mrs. Glisson put in with wifely zeal; "he made the bishopric. Cecil never thought of himself or his own comfort. He went up and down the country preaching like an apostle; and he collected all the funds with his magnetic eloquence. Then they offered him the see; but he didn't want to take it. He said his heart was more at home among his poor people in the Black Country: he would not desert his chain-makers. —Now, you know you did, Cecil.—But the Prime Minister insisted; and in the end he took it."

"After promising me, Olive, you must remember," the Bishop continued, "that he would transfer me to Wolverhampton as soon as that projected diocese is constituted. I made this one for Reading, you see, Sir Edward, with its enormous biscuit factories; I take an interest in my people there; but my heart is always with the puddlers and the chain-makers."

"And he was killing himself at Cradley," Evelyn put in; "and if he hadn't been sent here to vegetate by the Thames for a year or two, in peace, he'd have died in harness. I told the Prime Minister so, and he said to me: 'Miss Glisson, I know your father. He's a willing horse, and will work himself to death. He needs a curb, not a spur. We'll give him Dorchester for a year or two to quiet him. He'll *have* to rest there, comparatively, and it will do his health good. By and by, if he's good, he may go back to his chain-makers. Or at least, we'll promise

him that he shall, to pacify him.' For my part,
I hope we shall stop here always. I just love
this dear place; and I don't want to go back
to that beastly Cradley."

The Bishop smiled. " My dear," he said not
unkindly, " I cannot be expected to regulate the
acceptance or rejection of the work cut out for
me by your personal preferences. I must go
wherever I think I can be most useful."

" Papa's so dreadfully in earnest," Evelyn
added. " He takes bishoping seriously. If I
were a bishop, I'd go in for chasubles. But Papa
takes it out in episcopal supervision. He's so
full of its being a man's duty, however he gets
thrown into any walk of life, to do the best he
can in it."

The Bishop's brow clouded. " Yes," he repeated slowly; " however he gets thrown into
it. If chance makes you a sailor, be a sailor with
a will. If chance makes you—I mean, if Providence makes you a bishop, by whatever strange
steps, be a bishop with a will, and try to make
the best of it."

" Now, Cecil dear, I will not let you say, ' by
whatever strange steps,' " Mrs. Glisson interrupted. " There never was anyone so absurdly
modest as my husband, Sir Edward. He has
risen in the Church purely by dint of his own hard

work and his devotedness of purpose; and he always talks as if he were there by chance, and had dropped into a bishopric through a hole in the ceiling. Isn't that so, Cecil?"

The Bishop started. He was in a deep reverie. Her words had roused again that eternal remorse. Could no amount of well-doing atone for the way he had climbed into the fold by stealth like a thief in the night? After thirty years of outer conformity and hard work for the office he had assumed by chance, was he not yet a clergyman?

CHAPTER XVI.

"CECIL is in a brown study," Mrs. Glisson remarked in an undertone to Sir Edward. "He often gets so. I sometimes think he has worked too hard in both ways,—at clerical work and in his library." They had strolled out into the garden through the open French window, and Mrs. Glisson was pacing the lawn, hatless, in the warm June twilight. "You know, my husband had not the usual advantages of a university education; and when he began to take seriously to clerical work—other than missionary work, I mean—he felt the want of deeper knowledge. The consequence was, being a very thorough man, he set about studying hard at theological literature; and he worked in so many ways together—at the Fathers, you know——"

"I beg your pardon," Sir Edward put in, interrupting her and looking puzzled. "The Fathers? What Fathers?"

Mrs. Glisson smiled. She had helped her husband so long in his editions of Jerome and Cyril that patristic literature was to her quite familiar. " Oh, the Fathers of the Church, you know," she answered with a little apologetic wave of her hand towards the figure of the retreating Bishop, who stood gazing at the spot where Birinus had baptised the gentleman with the unpronounceable name. " My husband is much interested in them—St. Augustine and St. Ambrose and St. Gregory, don't you know; he has worked much at all of them. But then, at the same time, he was working at his Comparative Grammar of the Melanesian Languages, and at his evangelising labour among the Queensland immigrants, and at so many other things. Then again later, when he was doing so much for the Cradley chainmakers, he was also engaged on his Epistles of St. Cyril. People will tell you it was his Cradley work that got him made Canon and then Bishop; but Mr. Gladstone told me himself one main reason for his appointment was that he thought so highly of my husband's Hellenistic Concordance to the Synoptic Gospels."

" That was extremely gratifying!" Sir Edward exclaimed, with heavy dignity, beginning to think the Bishopess almost as serious as the Bishop. The Bishopina, indeed, was the only member of the family he could quite comprehend.

What sort of Gospel a synoptic might be he hadn't the faintest notion. As he remarked to Lady Colbeck the moment he got safe home again, Matthew, Mark, Luke, and John were good enough for him, and he didn't much care to know any new ones.

" Papa does work too hard," the Bishopina put in. She was of a mundane nature. " That's what makes him so moody. He's the dearest father any girl ever had; but sometimes when I go into his study in the morning, to ask him some question, he's sitting there mooning, with Cyril or somebody open on the table before him, and looking up at the ceiling, as if he was waiting for inspiration, so that he doesn't even know I'm there till I've spoken three times to him."

" He seems unduly absorbed," Sir Edward admitted. " Such an onerous position."

" Too many irons in the fire, poor dear," Evelyn responded with youthful frankness of criticism. To a bishop's daughter, even a bishop is human. Rococo, but human.

" I think you said he began life as a missionary," Sir Edward interposed. " Odd beginning for such an end. Not exactly the place most of our bishops come from." He was an emphatic man, and he rapped out his remarks with manufacturing jerkiness.

Mrs. Glisson sat down on the garden seat and began a glowing account of dear Cecil's early difficulties and how by earnestness, energy, and pure singleness of spirit he had gradually overcome them. She did not add that whatever he had done she had helped him to do; that was not Olive Glisson's way; she worshipped her husband, and she gave him the glory. "He's not an ornamental bishop," she said. "He has worked hard all his life. And now I'm afraid his hard work is beginning to tell upon him."

"He wants rest," Evelyn put in. "Sir Edward, I wish he could have accepted your invitation to go yachting to Norway."

"I'm not so sure of that," her mother answered. "On a yacht, he would have been idle. I often fancy, Evelyn, Papa is best when he has most to do. Since we've been here at Dorchester and he has had time to think, it seems to me he has worried much more than he used to do at Cradley. The chain-makers were good for him. He is happiest when he is bearing other people's troubles. If he feels he is doing good, that makes him happiest of anything."

Meanwhile, the Bishop, strolling slowly by himself, had paused by the brink, with his gaitered legs in the episcopal attitude of close attention, and was gazing into the baptismal stream of Birinus. He was trying his best to fix his attention upon those schools at Wallingford. They were sorely needed. And he loved to do good, as Olive had said of him. Two lines of an Elizabethan dramatist often seemed to help him; Ford put them into Jane Shore's mouth, but they served for him equally:

> " Although my good can not redeem my ill
> Yet to do good I will remember still."

He sat down by the brink, where Birinus had stood so many centuries before, and gazed again into the water. The long reflection of the trees on the opposite bank fell half across the river. Something that night made it all come back to him: he seemed to see his past life in the flickers of the beech-trees. He thought how he had gone away from Sydney, with Mr. Strong's commission, to preach down the labour traffic in all the towns of Australia. He thought how Olive's strength of character had helped him to do it. He recalled those crowded days, when he poured forth streams of eloquent denunciation on Sundays and holidays, and gave up his nights to diligent study of Greek and of the Melanesian tongue he was supposed to have learned long before at Temuka.

Then the rest recurred in all its long order.

He saw himself working hard to make a home for Olive—as soon as he thought he was enough of a parson to bear the daily scrutiny of a parson's daughter. How eagerly he had thrown himself into the task of denouncing the horrors he had seen with his own eyes; how he had worked with a will not to disgrace the name he had taken upon him by so strange a set of accidents! He succeeded at last in his efforts at breaking down the worst evils of the hateful slave-traffic, and then was appointed Government inspector and chaplain to the immigrants in Queensland. Sent to England finally, five years after he married Olive, he had come in fear and trembling, on a missionary trip, alarmed at every turn lest in London or Liverpool some sailor who had been a shipmate might see and recognise him. But gradually, these earlier terrors wore away. His metamorphosis was too complete. Twice he had met shipmates who gazed at him and went their way, unsuspicious; it was clear they never dreamt of recognising Tom Pringle the seaman in the close-shaven, clerically dressed man who stood before them.

His missionary trip was an immense success; his native gift of eloquence excited attention in England; and his own Society interested itself in finding him a parish in the Black Country, where it thought he might be more useful to it than in Queensland or Sidney. Cecil Glisson—as he now called himself—accepted the change with a certain passive calm which had become habitual with him since his total loss of his own personality. Eager always to escape from his torturing thoughts by plunging into work, he had thrown himself body and soul into the service of the chain-makers, and had succeeded in greatly alleviating the hardships of their condition. He had preached the gospel of a fair wage, and had not been so studious of literary grace as of convincing his hearers. So, step by step, Olive always assisting, he had worked his way up, without thought of self, to a canonry and a bishopric, rather by honest hard work than by cultivating what is known as clerical influence.

Yet at each upward step, his life grew ever more and more unendurable to him. Had he been a really bad man, like Blackburne, the Buccaneer Bishop of the eighteenth century, he would not have felt it so deeply. Had he been a complete unbeliever, he might only have been impressed by the moral wrong of his deception. But what made it worst was that he was now in essence a churchman and an ecclesiologist.

At the outset, to be sure, the Tom Pringle

who was now practically no more had possessed just an ordinary sailor's modicum of Christian doctrine. In a vague and careless way he had passively accepted the religion of his fathers, without concerning himself much as to its details or its formularies. He thought it was all true, but that it was the business of clergymen. Still, he was by nature a hard worker; and once turned by chance into the outer show of a parson, a parson he had become, to all intents and purposes, save those of the sacerdotalist. His standpoint was now that of the historically minded Anglican. He was never one of those modern philosophic clergymen who generously condescend to patronise Christianity. He believed—and trembled. And the very fact that intellectually he took a serious view of the priestly functions made the knowledge that in reality he was not a priest at all more and more alarming to him.

So he stood gazing at the trees that flickered in the water where Birinus had introduced Christianity into Wessex with a vague sort of wish that Birinus could come back with a private ordination to remove secretly the blot on his own episcopal scutcheon.

"Let us go back to the Bishop," Mrs. Glisson said, looking towards him. "I never like to leave him alone when he falls into one of these reveries."

They strolled back, still talking. "Yes, it is an unusual career," Mrs. Glisson said. "Few bishops have seen so many varied phases of life. But then, my husband is so clever, so earnest, so hard-working. You should have seen the way he rode all round Queensland, from station to station, looking after his blackfellows."

"And could he speak their language?" Sir Edward asked, as they reached the spot where the Bishop was standing. He had the usual exaggerated respect of half-educated men for mere linguistic attainments.

The Bishop answered for himself, looking up suddenly from his dream at the touch of his wife's hand. "Oh, yes, I spoke their language quite fluently; I speak it still. I learnt it while I was labouring among them in Northern Queensland."

"But you knew it before, Cecil," Mrs. Glisson interposed, correcting him. "You spoke it, of course, on Temuka."

The Bishop's face flushed fiery red. He seldom allowed himself these verbal slips, though he avoided them as far as possible by vague generalities; for a lie direct was intensely distasteful to him. "Ah yes, on Temuka," he answered. "Yes —of course—on Temuka. But then, though the language is essentially the same throughout all the islands, the dialects differ so much, you know. It's all a question of dialect." And he looked up appealingly.

"He was a missionary at Temuka," Mrs. Glisson went on, "before I met him. Evelyn has told you the story of his capture and his marvellous rescue from the piratical labour vessel. Most romantic, isn't it?"

"But Papa will never talk about Temuka," Evelyn put in once more, in her irreverent manner. "A bishop has never a Past, of course, or I should almost believe Papa's Past was on Temuka. He so carefully avoids saying anything about it. My own belief is, he was glad to get away from it."

"Evelyn, my dear, how *can* you talk so?" Mrs. Glisson exclaimed, horrified. "Why, he was longing to get back, and if I hadn't insisted that he mustn't waste the great talents which Providence had given him on a single small island —hide them in a napkin, so to speak—I believe he would have gone back and lived and died there."

"That's just it," Evelyn insisted, with a mischievous voice—she was no respecter of bishops —"That was his Past, you may be certain. She was waiting for him on the island. Having got rid of the Past with a violent effort, and married you, dear, he naturally doesn't care to dwell upon the subject. I always notice he declines to say much about anything that occurred before he first met you, Mother. Isn't that so, Daddy?" And she looked up at him quizzically. For Evelyn, you will perceive, was a very modern young lady.

The Bishop's face wore an anxious expression as he stooped down and kissed her. " My child," he said evasively, " if you rattle on like this, Sir Edward will think I have failed egregiously in one main apostolic requirement in a bishop, ' One that ruleth well his own house, having his children in subjection with all gravity.' You are distinctly lacking in gravity, Evelyn."

He said it half playfully, but Mrs. Glisson saw a shadow of pain cross his face, and hastened to turn aside the conversation into some lighter channel. She called attention to the copper beeches.

" Yes, you have a lovely place here," Sir Edward admitted, firing off his pompous commonplaces with a ponderous air of profound originality. " Nature is very charming. Her works are all so complete. Their minuteness! their beauty! A shell now! or a flower! The perfection of her smallest handicraft, it often strikes me,

Mrs. Glisson, contrasts marvellously with the roughness of man's best productions. A fragment of Manchester piece-goods under the microscope, for example——"

The Bishop turned upon him suddenly. " It . is the *im*perfection of nature that oftener puzzles *me*," he said with a real sense of mystery. " Her cruelty, her tyranny, her armed emphatic lawlessness. Look at that fly in the twilight—joyous, airy, unconscious of fate: and, swoop, it has disappeared into the gaping beak of a swift. A little thing, you say. Yes, but why should it suffer *at all?* The origin of evil has troubled the theologians: it is the origin of suffering that troubles me. How can a beneficent and omnipotent Being permit, even for a time, this reign of pain, of physical agony, of mental torture? I cannot understand it—that what revolts man's moral sense should be permitted, nay carefully provided for, by man's Maker! "

Sir Edward looked up sharply. He was positively shocked. That a bishop should permit himself to think like this! And that he should presume to see two sides of a question! Sir Edward didn't like it: for he had always been a fervent admirer of the commonplace.

CHAPTER XVII.

TO GO OR NOT TO GO.

WHEN the Bishop was left alone with Mrs. Glisson that evening, the watchful wife saw at once from his face that something had gone wrong with him. She could read his expression like an open book. "Well, Cecil," she asked, "what was this business of Sir Edward's that is troubling you, darling?"

The Bishop sighed deeply. "I knew it would come," he replied in a sad slow voice. "Sooner or later, I knew it would come. They have written more than once; and as I refuse by letter, they've now sent down a personal ambassador to speak to me."

"Who have sent?" Mrs. Glisson asked.

The Bishop paused again for a second. Then he jerked it out with a wrench. "Why, the Liverpool orphanage. They want me to go down and open a new school for them."

"Well," Mrs. Glisson answered quietly. "Why don't you say *yes?*"

The Bishop gave a hasty gesture of dislike and despair with one hand. " If you knew how I hate that place, Olive! I can't bear to go near it."

" I know that, Cecil. And though I can never imagine why, I won't bother you any more to tell me the reason. *You* feel it: that is enough for me. Still, couldn't you make the effort—just this once? Perhaps if you went there you would find it wasn't as bad after all as you expected. Do try, for my sake, Cecil." And her hand sought his soothingly.

" Olive, when you talk like that, you don't know how you lacerate me! I can't bear not to do what you ask me in this way. And yet—I can't go. You haven't a notion how I shrink from it."

" I have, darling; I see it: but I feel you ought. Cecil, I don't like even to hint such a thing to you, it is so wholly different from your real character; but doesn't it strike you that if you persistently stop away, people will imagine you're ashamed of having been brought up at an orphanage? *I* know, of course, that such an idea could never enter your dear head; but the world doesn't know it, and it will think you snobbish."

The Bishop snapped one hand impatiently

again. "The world, the world!" he said with an unwonted touch of irony in his tone. "The dear, good world! For each of us, some hundred or so of foolish and ill-natured gossips! Have I ever minded the world? Do I care what people think? Have I ever cared what people thought about anything? Am I not here to-day just because I have always persistently disregarded what the foolish world cackled, and gone straight for what I believed to be right and justice?"

"Yes, I know that, dear; nobody knows it better than I do: you fought for the chain-makers against rank and capital, when everybody said you were ruining your prospects; and you answered: 'Let them be ruined, but be just to the chain-makers.' Nobody respects you for all that as I respect you, dearest. Still," she lifted his hand in hers and soothed it gently; "this case is somewhat different. It is only a personal repugnance you have to overcome here; and if people think you won't go because you are too proud to acknowledge your connection with the institution that brought you up, that will surely tend to lessen your influence for good in the diocese and the country. Think of all that, darling. While you were only a canon, I never urged you hard; but now that you are a bishop, I do think you ought really to make an effort and go to them. The orphanage is naturally proud of having produced a bishop; you should let people see you are not ashamed to own it."

The Bishop folded his hands on his apron, leaned back in his chair, and closed his eyes wearily. Strange to say, it was not at first that the deception had cost him dear, but at last. The longer he lived, the higher he rose in life, the more earnestly he strove to do such good as he could in his false position, the more terribly did the dead past rise up and accuse him.

His own innate truthfulness and honesty were his worst enemies now. A wickeder man would have gone down to the orphanage boldly and brazened it out with lies; but the Bishop shrank from lies with an honest shrinking. It wasn't merely the fear of detection that disturbed him. Who, after all these years, was likely to know into what manner of man the Cecil Glisson of the orphanage might by this time have developed? No; what he really dreaded was the deception and the pretence. He could not bear to go down to the place where he had never lived, and pretend to remember the things he had never seen. So he leaned back in his chair and murmured feebly, once more: " If you knew how hateful it all was to me, Olive, you would never ask me."

"Yes, yes, dear; I *do* know; and I can understand that in those days the boys may have been roughly treated; I always see that you have the utmost repugnance to talking of your boyhood there; and I feel sure it is because you think the system then was cruel. But all that must be quite changed by now. The world moves. You needn't be afraid of opening their new school because you believe the lads are ill-treated nowadays. Sir Edward was talking to me about that matter just now, and he says a jollier or healthier set of little fellows he never saw in his life—perfect pictures of merry happy-go-lucky English schoolboys."

The Bishop started. "Olive, dearest," he cried, "I never once suggested that the system was cruel. I deny it. I disclaim it. It distresses me that you should hint it. I—I never heard one word of complaint against the school from —from any boy who was educated there." As a matter of fact, he recollected that the real Cecil Glisson, the Cecil Glisson whose bones lay bleaching beneath the Pacific waves, had always spoken in the most affectionate terms of the orphanage and its masters. "No, dearest one, it isn't that. I should feel it most unjust if any-one carried away the impression that I declined to go because I bore any ill-will to the institution." He felt he ought to add, as Cecil Glisson: "On the contrary, I'm most grateful to it;" but the words stuck in his throat. He altered them slowly to: "On the contrary, I see no reason to doubt that every boy who was brought up there has good grounds for gratitude."

Mrs. Glisson read in his face the struggle and the reservation. But she did not pursue that part of the subject. She was content to know that some internal feeling made Cecil unwilling to talk freely with her about his youth. So she altered the mode of attack.

"At any rate, dear," she said, "you must feel that your stopping away now is open to misconstruction, and that the misconstruction does wrong both to the orphanage itself and to your own chances of usefulness. People will say: 'Here is Dr. Glisson, who sets up to be the democratic bishop, the people's bishop, the poor man's bishop; yet he's ashamed to own the orphanage that bred him.' And that must do harm in the end to every cause you have most at heart, mustn't it?"

The Bishop flared up. "Have I ever been ashamed of anything like that?" he asked, petulantly. "You are unjust to me, Olive. Have I not always said I crept into the church by the smallest of side doors, and that I desire no pretence of social distinction. I hate it when they My-Lord me. Nobody that I know of My-Lorded the apostles. But this is quite different; this is a personal and sentimental objection. I'll give them a subscription, if they wish, with all my heart; but I can't endure to go and open their school for them."

.Mrs. Glisson desisted. "Very well, dear," she answered with a disappointed look. "If you feel it so strongly, it would be wrong of me to urge it."

Her face was distressed. The Bishop saw it and groaned inwardly. For Olive had become to him a perfect religion. He knew in his heart that it was she who had made him; she who had developed whatever there was of strong and good within him; and he hated to distress her. "If you look like that," he cried, "I must do violence to myself and go down to Liverpool."

"No, darling; you mustn't do it if you do it on that ground. I couldn't bear to feel I was sending you anywhere against your better judgment."

"It's not my better judgment; it's my feelings, Olive."

"Well, against your feelings, then, Cecil."

The Bishop paced the room, agitated. He reflected for some minutes. Then he made up his mind. " Perhaps you're right, dear," he said slowly, bending over her and kissing her. " Indeed, when are you not right? I see abstention lays me open to a painful misconception. I suppose I must go; though few things have cost me such a wrench of late years. . . . It's a most painful visit to pay. But, Olive, I will pay it. You may tell Sir Edward to-morrow morning I've reconsidered my determination, and will run down next week, if Providence permits, to open the new school at the Liverpool orphanage."

It would cost him dear, but he could not bear to differ from Olive.

CHAPTER XVIII.

LOVE UP TO DATE.

Next morning at eleven, a little above Day's Lock, a tall young man in a Canadian canoe sat paddling about disconsolately. He had the irresolute, dispirited, watchful air of one who has come to time to an appointment and finds the other party to the bargain absent. His face at once betrayed the undergraduate. But he was a nice-looking specimen of that aggressive class, in an Oxford blazer; and he kept paddling to one side of the river and then to the other, glancing first at his watch and then up and down stream with the unmistakable look of a person who says to himself: " Why doesn't she come? I'm sure I made no blunder about the hour."

He continued reconnoitring the side-streams for several minutes together, and then, evidently dejected, ran himself into a thick bed of iris-leaves by the bank, and assumed an attitude of profound melancholy. Suddenly, another canoe shot quick round the corner, and a young girl approached, paddling well and deftly with an air of assured mastery of the craft. She was a slight, dark girl, with abundant black hair; not exactly pretty, but with haunting eyes, and a wistful gipsy air that was better than prettiness: she wore a loose pink blouse and a hat with wild roses. The man's face and attitude altered at once as she appeared. In a moment, he was alert, attentive, eager, smiling. He paddled out to meet her down a backwater to which it was evident they were both well accustomed. The girl's face was aglow. They came up with one another under shelter of a mass of tall purple loose-strife, which hid them from observation from the field beside them.

" Well, Alex, you thought I was never coming, I suppose," she broke out, drawing close to him. " Now, don't look at your watch; it was all my fault. You said half past ten. But I couldn't get away earlier. It's just this beastly bishoping. A certain Sir Edward Colbeck, who is something or other in iron or cotton down in Warrington or elsewhere, came to the Palace last night to persuade Daddy he ought to go somewhere and open something he doesn't want to open—oysters, or orphanages, or ginger-beer or something; and Mums was on Sir Edward's side; she's always in favour of Daddy fulfilling his duty in that station of life, etc., etc., as per the Church Catechism; and Daddy said *no*, but Mums stuck to it like a leech: and the upshot of it is Daddy's going, of course; so there's an end of it. But after breakfast, Mums said: 'Evelyn, you must take Sir Edward through the grounds;' and I tried to cry off; but Mums was blind as a bat; it's the way of mothers; and I couldn't get away. And Sir Edward's a bore; and he talked on and on, and made himself middle-aged agreeable. And the consequence was, I couldn't give him the slip till just this moment; and if Mums finds I've gone off now, she'll be in a state of mind about it; because she wants me to keep Sir Edward from worrying Daddy while he's seeing these people about the clergyman at Reading who has run away from his parish. So *that's* why I'm late. And you mustn't blame me for it, but set it down to the bothering old diocese."

Alex gazed at her admiringly as she turned on him with a defiant air. " I couldn't blame you for anything, darling," he said; " and of course . I see it wasn't your fault. But I'm happy now you've come. I was *so* afraid you couldn't get away at all; and I'd taken a pony-cart over from Oxford, of course—the last time, I'm afraid, for I'm dead broke now, and can't afford any more pony-carts over this term, let alone the Schools beginning on Monday. And it would have been horrid to miss you."

Evelyn drove her canoe a little farther into the loose-strife. The purple clump rose round them like a thicket, screening them effectually both from the river-side and the shore. "Well, here I am, at last," she answered, with a bewitching smile, for she *was* bewitching when she was not provoking. "I managed to give Sir Edward the slip while he was talking to Mums; and off I darted to the canoe, and I've paddled down so fast that I've no doubt by this time I'm unbecomingly hot; but—I dare say you'll excuse it."

She *was* hot, but tempting. The undergraduate drew his canoe quite close to hers, and executed a manœuvre which only persons accustomed to Canadian canoes can permit themselves with impunity. He leaned over the edge, caught Evelyn in his arms, and clasped her tight for a moment. The sound that followed is one for which typography has as yet no symbol. Evelyn flushed rosy red and recovered equilibrium with some little difficulty. "There, you wicked boy," she said, "you've nearly upset me!" But she did not seem seriously displeased for all that, nor did she withdraw her canoe with more than a formal protest.

Alex Thornbury stood off at paddle's length

and surveyed her.   As she sat there, flushed with excitement, in the first full flower of opening womanhood, she looked as beautiful as her mother had looked thirty years before, but with a stranger and more elusive type of beauty.   Her great weird eyes thrilled him.   She had the conscious pride of youth, too, which sat on her not ungracefully; and her air was high-bred, though her phrases were so modern and sometimes so slangy.   In one word, she was the typical Ibsenite, the high-spirited over-strung girl of the later nineteenth century—a type which our mothers would have considered unladylike, but which our sons agree in finding most pleasantly piquant.

"You must make the most of me to-day, Evey," he said, with the quiet presumption of an assured lover; "for I shan't be able to come at all next week.   I shall be in the Schools all the week—examinations, don't you know; and then, as I shall be sitting over papers all day long, from nine to five, there won't be a chance even if I walked over to see you."

"You could come in the evenings, couldn't you?" Evelyn asked in response, gazing eagerly and wistfully.

Alex shook his head.   "No, that won't work," he answered.   "Out of the Schools at five; well, say even I missed Hall, and didn't get any dinner, I couldn't be over here much before eight or nine. Then it would be late for you to get out; and besides, I should have to be back in college by eleven. I'm gated this term at eleven you know, on account of that row about the Tutor's window. So it wouldn't be possible."

Evelyn pouted just enough to look engaging. "What a nuisance," she cried. "Shall I have to go a whole week without seeing you?"

"It *is* a deprivation, isn't it?" Alex answered.

"You conceited boy! You shouldn't take that for granted. Though it's true, for all that." And she nodded at him deliciously.

Alex coloured to the ears. "Oh, I didn't mean for you," he said. "I'm not so coxy as that. I meant for myself, darling. But there's really no help for it. Besides, you know, I *ought* to do well in the Schools; *our* future depends upon it. Unless I get a good class, there'll be no chance of our marrying for oh, ever and ever so long."

"What has coming to see me got to do with that? I thought a woman's love was supposed to be an incentive—isn't that the word they always use in novels?—an incentive to a man to do his very best in everything. You horrid creature—" but she drew a little nearer again—" you ought to say that you feel coming here inspires you; that it stimulates your efforts; that you'd willingly walk over every night by moonlight and see me at all risks, in order to be able to answer the questions ten times better in the morning.—There, don't do that again; oh, Alex, take care; if you pull me so far I'm sure I'll go over."

" No, you won't," Alex answered, releasing her, after an interval which I can only represent by a series of full stops. " But you know very well you're talking nonsense. The driving-power of love is as true as gospel; it's made me read this term every minute of my time—when I wasn't coming over here; it's made me read like a steam engine, if steam engines do read: I never read before as I've read since you've been so sweet to me. Still, ·the driving power has its limits. It must be applied scientifically. You know as well as I do that if I come over and see you every night, I won't be able to think of a blessed thing all next day except how much I love you. Now it's no use telling the examiners in Greek hexameters, ' I love Evelyn Glisson; she's the dearest, sweetest, provokingest girl that ever was born.' They'd only remark in their bleak way that *that* wasn't the piece set for translation into tragic senarii—and that 'provokingest' was ungrammatical—though it's true, for all that."

"Oh, Alex, don't; you hurt my arm so!"

"Still, you must see for yourself it's no good trying that way. I've got to go into the Schools all day, and read up the subject for the next morning all night. *That's* the way the driving-power of love acts on me, Miss Glisson. (I call you Miss Glisson by way of variety.) It makes me work like a horse—for your sake, Evey."

"But Mr. Beddingley was saying a man in examination ought never to read at night. He ought to throw it all off, as soon as the day's work is over, and go out on the river. I call that common sense. And *I* should think that for throwing it all off there's nothing on earth to equal——"

"When was Beddingley over here?"

"Oh, my, who's jealous now? Mr. Beddingley was over here yesterday, sir, by Mums's invitation. Such a good young man, Mr. Beddingley! So very well connected! His uncle's a judge; and haven't you observed that judges' nephews invariably marry into bishopy families? There, I've done it again! Mums says I mustn't say *bishopy*, but episcopal; you know, she hasn't found out yet that bishops are out of date: she tells me *bishopy* gives away the show, or words to that effect; is unbecoming my father's daughter; but, do I *look* episcopal?" And to do her justice, she certainly didn't.

"No; you look a charming heathen. What did Beddingley want?"

"Me, I suppose; though I didn't ask him. Mums thinks I'm incorrigible; but even *I* don't say to a young man when he calls: ' Pray what have you come for?' "

" I hate Beddingley."

"*That's* not episcopal. It's not even Christian. You should love your enemies. And Mr. Beddingley isn't an enemy; he says he's a friend of yours. He's an excellent young man. I know that for certain, because Mums is always telling me so, ten times a day. He will go into the church,—the church loves the middling—and as soon as he's old enough, and in priest's orders, the Lord Chancellor will stick him into a nice fat living. He will deserve it, Mr. Beddingley. There's an oozing goodness about him that shows at a glance he's cut out for a parson. He will marry a wife after his own pattern, and become the parent of ten assorted offspring, all congenially and stupidly commonplace. He will interest himself in foreign missions and in old women's rheumatism. He will make contributions to theological literature. I hate such young men. There! who says I'm episcopal?"

"Oh, Evey, if Mrs. Glisson could hear you?"

"She hears me often enough, dear old Mums. She thinks it's original sin coming out in me. Not that she *really* minds. Mums is no more bishopy at heart than Daddy and I are. And Daddy is only an incidental Bishop. But she has more sense of the dignity of the episcopal position than we. You see, she was brought up in a clergyman's family; while I was brought up in Daddy's; and *he's* no clergyman. It did him heaps of good being among the blackfellows when he was young—took a lot of the starch out of him."

Alex gazed admiration again. "Do you know, Evey," he said, looking hard at her, "I love you for your lawlessness. You're the incarnation of an age of revolt. I *am* so glad you never went to Cambridge. It would have spoilt you utterly."

"Oh, I don't think even Cambridge would have made much out of *me*. It would have run off me like water off a something-or-other's back. A duck, is it? thank you. Resist the higher education, and it will flee from you. When Daddy first spoke to me about going to Cambridge, I said 'Get thee behind me, Girton,' and it gat thee behind me; at least, that was the last I heard of it."

"You provoking angel, I do declare, I love you more——"

"Now, no Georgey-porgeying! I won't be Georgey-porgeyed. I'm sure little Beddingley would always Georgey-porgey!"

"Then Beddingley doesn't interest you?"

"Silly boy to ask such a thing. He disinterests me altogether. There, don't look so critical. We say 'disinterested,' so I suppose we can say say 'disinterests me.' That's logical, isn't it? Women are always logical."

"You wouldn't like to marry a parson?"

"Oh, my, what a question! Don't you see me doing it? Was I cut out to teach in a Sunday school and to organise Dorcas meetings? Why, Dorcas herself died of it—bored to death, I expect, and sorry enough to be resuscitated for a second edition over again of the same sort of dulness. I wouldn't marry a parson if there wasn't another man left alive on earth. I'd sooner run away with—with a dentist or an organist."

"It's all very well laughing at organists, Evey; but what do you think I'm to turn to when I've taken my degree? I shall probably be a schoolmaster. Remember, we can't marry till

I've got on enough to ask a bishop's blessing."

Evelyn grew suddenly graver. "Well, I had an idea the other day," she said, looking wise. "If only I dare tell Daddy—not that I'm afraid of *him*, of course; but there's Mums to think of. It's this; they say Daddy is the only bishop in the whole batch whose recommendation for an Inspector of Schools is *not* a positive disadvantage to a candidate. But Daddy's such a favourite at the Education Office, or whatever they call the place, that if *he* recommends a man they almost always appoint him. Now, my idea is that after you've taken your degree, I should present you to Daddy one day and say: 'Dads, this is the man I'm going to marry; and we've got nothing to marry on; and we object on principle to long engagements, as wearing to the feelings; and we want you to get him an Inspector-of-Schoolship.' Rather noble, isn't it?"

"Intensely noble," Alex answered with alacrity. "As noble as a Marquis; and Marquises, you know, are always Most Noble. In fact, an idea worthy of your intelligence, Evey. The worst of it is, I must get a First for that; and I'm so terribly weak in my Politics, I'm afraid."

"Politics? why, what have politics got to do with it?" Evelyn exclaimed, surprised. "You don't mean to say they won't give you a First because you're a thingumbob, do you?"

Alex smiled. "No, not because I'm a thingumbob," he answered. "Thingumbobs, as such, are eligible for the highest offices in the university, just the same as what-you-may-call-its. But I mean Aristotle's Politics, don't you know; it's one of the books one has to take up for greats. And I'm so beastly bad at it."

"Oh, *you'll* pull through," Evelyn responded, with a girl's confidence in her lover's ability to do anything that is expected of him. "You'll get a First all right. Mr. Beddingley said yesterday: 'There's no doubt about Thornbury. He's safe of his First; he's read so hard since Christmas.' And I knew what had made you; so there, sir."

"But, Evelyn, I say, that's a splendid idea about the Inspectorship of Schools!"

"*I* said, Inspector-of-schoolship, which I venture to think much more neat and appropriate."

"So it is, of course; it's the right idiom, obviously; only, idioms are generally made by idiots, and when a clever person like you strikes out the right one offhand, one's afraid to use it. But, Inspectorship or Schoolship, it's a noble idea; we must work that, you know; why, then, we might get married in rather less than no time! "

" Really? "

" Yes, really."

" Then, my dear old boy, go in and win! Get a First, and it's done, as conjurors always tell one. Daddy and the Education Office won't know what it is to have a quiet night till they've given you the appointment. I'll nobble Sir Nathaniel: he's a dear old friend of mine. Church schools; schedule C; oh, I know all about it; I've been looking it up to-day in Daddy's School Manager's Assistant, a Complete Digest of the Education Act and the Revised Code, for the Use of the Unmitigated Old Bores who sit upon the Committees. I dare say I haven't got the title ' with textual accuracy,' as Daddy would say; but it's near enough for all practical purposes." And she looked up at him saucily.

She had taken off her hat. He ran his hand through her hair. " I love you, Evey," he said. " I wonder why I love you! "

She laughed a pleased laugh. " Interrogate your consciousness! "

He paused and reflected. " I think," he said, " it is, because you're a double acrostic."

CHAPTER XIX.

THE EPISCOPATE STOOPS.

THE episode of the opening was fixed to take place on the following Tuesday. By Thursday of the week before the date arranged for it, the poor harassed Bishop, turning things over in his mind, this way and that, arrived all at once at a notable resolution. It was clear he could not go down to the orphanage where according to the authorities he had been bred and taught, without the slightest idea what manner of place it was. He must sally forth on an exploring expedition to Liverpool, incog., before trusting himself to make a speech of effusive gratitude and misplaced humility at the opening of the new school where he had never been educated.

But what a sordid, what a hateful, what an undignified necessity—a necessity that revolted all the manhood within him; for whatever else he was, the man who had once been Tom Pringle remained a man to the end, in spite of his apron. He had preached down coal-mines, and chummed with chain-makers, and helped puddlers at their work, and fought drunken navvies, and shown himself in fifty unconventional ways a muscular Christian. But this surreptitious creeping about in disguise, like a thief or a detective, was wholly repugnant to him. Still, he had made his bed and he must lie on it. Or rather, as he said bitterly to himself more than once, a chance moment had made it, and a lifetime must lie on it.

He opened the study door with a consciously furtive air, ill-disguised under a pretence of transparent candour, for he was a mighty poor dissembler. "Watkins," he said to his servant, in the most casual voice he could summon, "do you happen to have kept that old suit I used to wear at Cradley for visiting the chain-works?"

"Yes, my lord; it's in the box-room."

"Then bring it out, Watkins, and pack it in my Gladstone bag." His look was guilty. "I'm going down—to Birmingham." Birmingham was on the way, and he must change there to get on the North Western for Liverpool. He salved his conscience as usual with one of the verbal subterfuges he despised and hated.

"Yes, my lord. And what else shall I put in?"

The Bishop paused. "The usual things for

one night," he answered, hesitating. "And a coloured tie, if I have any. No, no; I shan't want one," he continued, reflecting after a moment that it was safer to buy one than to give himself away to his own man-servant. "Just the Cradley suit and the usual night things, Watkins."

"Yes, my lord," Watkins answered stolidly. He was too much accustomed to the eccentricities of "the slumming bishop," as his clergy called him, to feel or express much astonishment at these episcopal vagaries.

"And Watkins, tell Rees I shall want to be driven to the station to catch the 11.30. And when Mrs. Glisson comes home, say I was suddenly called away on pressing business connected with this forged orders question." That was, alas, too true. He need not tell a lie this time; though the case of forged orders which called him away had nothing to do with the clergyman at Reading."

"Yes, my lord," Watkins answered in the same impassive voice—the colourless voice of the trained man-servant who would answer "Yes, my lord," if you told him the moon was made of green cheese or commanded him to cut off the head of his grandmother.

With infinite loathing, the Bishop took the

next train to Birmingham. On his way thence to Liverpool, he managed to secure a solitary first class compartment; and during the longest unbroken run, changed his clothes in the carriage in terror, reappearing with a very workmanlike suit in place of his gaiters, and substituting a crush felt hat for his episcopal head-gear.

Arrived at Lime Street Station, he felt his difficulties thicken round him. It would be dangerous to proceed too openly to the orphanage, for if he let himself be seen, he might be recognised again in his episcopal dress on Tuesday. On the other hand, it would not do to skulk about too clandestinely with the air of one who would escape observation, and so run the risk of being apprehended by the police in his present masquerade on a charge of loitering with intent to commit a burglary. He split the difference; drove to a third-rate hotel, instead of the one he meant to patronise on Tuesday; and then lounged quietly round, with the aid of a map, to the place where the orphanage was marked as existing.

It would have been a disagreeable task for anybody; for a bishop, it was insupportable. In his working-man suit, he felt like a mountebank. The sense of skulking about those buildings in order to assume a familiarity with them which he did not really possess, was almost more than his honest heart could endure. For after all, his heart was still honest. He was a truthful man, utterly warped and turned aside from his own proper nature by one lasting error. He hoped, indeed, to avoid a lie direct, which his soul hated; but he hardly saw how he could succeed in avoiding a certain amount of prevarication. " Ah, here's the old school-room," he must say, with a tone of conviction and of ancient acquaintance; " and here's the dormitory. This is where the boys used to play rounders on half holidays; and that's the window erected in memory of the three poor fellows who were killed in the Crimea." All these details he must get up beforehand as far as possible; and to get them up he had but his unaided intelligence. To ask questions, he felt, would be absolutely fatal. The town hummed with affairs, but the Bishop disregarded them. He made his way straight to a straggling suburb.

He found the building, a gaunt brick block upon a windy hill-top, standing a mile or two from the centre, in a forbidding garden, with the usual desolate air of a great British charity. Its mien and aspect were strictly utilitarian. The gates stood open, thank heaven, and he walked in, unchallenged. As always happens on such occasions—'tis a human peculiarity—the work was behindhand, and all hands were impressed into the service making diligent efforts to get the building ship-shape for the date of the opening. It is the humour of contractors to put off everything till the last moment. Accustomed as he was to see his own name and office placarded, it still gave him a strange start to-day to read the notices on the gate, in large red type, " The New School House will be opened on Tuesday, June the 27th, by the Right Reverend the Lord Bishop of Dorchester." He feared to enter. If anybody were to see him now and then recognise him next week, what an appalling disclosure!

However, whatever else the Bishop was, he was a brave man, and he pushed his way in boldly. It was not his habit to quail or whimper. He walked round the building with a certain assured air in his upright carriage which secured him from enquiry. Even at the worst of times the Bishop respected himself. This was the old school-room, then; not a doubt about that; he could hear the hum and buzz of voices inside, the unmistakable drone of boys repeating rote-lessons. He measured it with the eye, length, breadth, and height, and observed its relation to the surrounding buildings. Then he scanned the bricks curiously. Yes, he should say from the colour they must have been laid for more than thirty years; probably forty; so that the room must have been there in the *other* Cecil Glisson's time; for since Cecil Glisson had been his own name now for more than a quarter of a century, he had grown to regard its original owner as merely " the other one."

Was he right in judging that this school-room was so old, though? Liverpool is a smoky place, and brick would discolour there quickly. These walls were certainly newer than those just to the right of them; not quite so new as those to the left beyond. A mistake on this matter would be,—not indeed quite conclusive, for so many years had passed since,—but, to say the least of it, suspicious. The Bishop recalled the blunders of the Tichborne claimant. He looked carefully from this point of view at every part of the building, except that now in progress. The new works he left intentionally out of consideration, so that they might strike him with as much unfamiliarity by comparison as possible.

Presently, he drew near the workmen's chief hut. The clerk of the works was there, holding a plan in his hand. The Bishop approached him and murmured in his suave episcopal manner: " Might I be permitted to glance at it? "

" Certainly, sir," the clerk answered; and that

sir struck cold into the Bishop's heart; he had expected rather to be addressed as *matc*, for he was clad as a working man on the borderland of the class—a foreman or its equivalent—and he was dimly aware that his voice had bewrayed him. "Thank you so much," he continued, trying his hardest to be gruff; but it was all in vain; for even Tom Pringle had had a soft and peculiarly gentle manner of speech, which was one of the first points Olive had noted and admired in him. And now that he was a bishop, his tones had the correct episcopal silveriness.

The clerk of the works pointed out some of the details. The Bishop pretended to look and listen; but his eyes were really elsewhere on other parts of the plan. For as good luck would have it, this was a small-scale elevation of the entire buildings, old and new, with their junctions of passages. More still, it had in its corner a ground plan of the orphanage, marking in red, blue, and black figures the dates of the various successive layers, so to speak. The Bishop glanced at these hastily, and took them in at a glance. Necessity is the mother of memory as well as of invention. He never knew before how well he could take in and carry away a plan; in two minutes, he had committed the whole thing to the tablets of his brain, and was prepared to recognise every part or not, exactly in proportion as it antedated or post-dated the real Cecil Glisson's sojourn in the institution.

"Thank you immensely," he said with a genuine sigh of relief to the clerk; for he had learnt from this chart by how little he had avoided one tremendous pitfall; the dubious school-room had *not* been there in Cecil Glisson's day at all; it was the middle one in time of three successive buildings; and it was begun in the year after Cecil Glisson went to the Theological College. Thank heaven, that particular Theological College had wholly failed in the struggle for existence between seminaries of budding parsons, and was now a retreat for decayed licensed victuallers; and therefore he would never be called upon to gush over an apocryphal stay in *that* building, at any rate!

So he said, "Thank you immensely," with a real touch of gratitude.

"Not at all, sir," the clerk answered, staring hard at him from head to foot, and beginning to wonder whether or not this smooth-voiced stranger was a gentlemanly burglar or a swell-mob pickpocket.

The Bishop ventured on a question. "Shall you be here on Tuesday?" he asked nervously after a moment's hesitation.

The clerk stared again and hesitated in turn. "Not *inside*," he answered. That was a relief, anyhow. Yet the Bishop began to wonder whether it would not be well for him to contract a sudden indisposition and telegraph regrets at the last moment to the committee. For the clerk had taken stock of him with a most suspicious scrutiny.

He returned to his shabby hotel not a little perturbed in soul. He was not quite sure that this unpleasant visit had not rather increased than lessened his difficulties.

CHAPTER XX.

THE LION'S MOUTH.

WORRY kills. As a matter of fact, through fatigue and worry, the Bishop was very far indeed from being well on the succeeding Monday. His head swam ominously.

"Olive, dear," he said to his wife when he got up in the morning, "I'm really afraid, after all, I shall have to telegraph and disappoint those Liverpool people. I feel really ill, more than a passing headache. I don't believe I shall be up to it."

"Well, of course, dear, if you're unable to go, you mustn't go," Mrs. Glisson answered, with a luminous platitude. "But at least we might set out and get as far as Liverpool. Then you could see how you are to-morrow. We can sleep to-night at the Adelphi; the Adelphi's so comfortable: and if you're no better in the morning, we can write and explain. Still, your little ailment will probably pass off; you know your head is almost always better for the change of a journey."

The Bishop groaned; but there was nothing for it but to obey. He was an obedient husband. He went to Liverpool, and, strange to say, felt better next morning, with the usual incredible incalculability of nervous troubles. And when the dreaded hour arrived, he opened the new school with great solemnity and dignity. Fortunately, he had little to say about the institution, himself, or his own supposed connection with it. The Mayor and the others did that part of the speechifying: they dilated on the pleasure it gave them to see that a Spiritual Peer in Dr. Glisson's exalted position had come originally from their own institution; they enlarged upon the fact that the Lord Bishop of Dorchester, in all his glory, was not ashamed now to own his indebtedness to their Orphan's Home; and they pointed the usual fallacious moral that every boy there present that day had it open to him to pursue a similar career of usefulness which might lead him at last, if not to so conspicuous and honoured a position, at least to high posts in the Church and Commonwealth. It is annoying to any man to have to sit still and hear himself thus publicly belauded; to the Bishop, under the circumstances, it was an unspeakable ordeal. Every now and again he caught Olive's eye and gave a profound sigh of impatient resignation.

Olive encouraged him silently. Without that wifely aid, he almost believed he must have risen in his place and protested openly.

For himself, when it came to his turn, the Bishop did little more than briefly allude to the much too kind and flattering things which the Mayor had said about him; and then passed on to a short and obviously heart-felt phrase about his own exceeding unworthiness. That was one of the little traits that had made Dr. Glisson the most popular of bishops; his real modesty was undeniable; consciousness of his false claim saved him at every turn from the besetting episcopal sin of self-complacency. To the orphanage he referred in safe generalities only; it was his stereotyped way of avoiding direct falsehood.

He said, with his silvery intonation, that every boy who had been educated in that Home must always look back to his sojourn there with pleasure and gratitude. If any inmate who owed his career of usefulness to the Institution where they were now assembled was ashamed in after life of the sheltering school which had made him what he was, that inmate showed a mean and contemptible spirit. Lads educated under this roof had recalled their boyhood with pride and delight beneath the starry splendours of the Southern Cross and among the waving palms and tree-ferns of the Pacific. (For he remembered what the real Cecil Glisson had told him.) No tie save the tie of parent and child could be closer than the link which bound the pupils of that school in almost filial piety to the Home that had proved itself a father to the fatherless. And never in a long life had he felt more profoundly thankful to have discharged the part he had been called upon to play than he should feel that night when he returned once more with the memory of this duty fulfilled to his home at Dorchester. He added a few general moral and religious platitudes—the inevitable stock-in-trade of an episcopal orator : and then, amid much applause, and with the usual ceremonies, he solemnly declared this institution open.

He did not, however, return that night to Dorchester Palace. Mrs. Glisson was so much alarmed at the strain he had obviously endured that she would not allow him to try the journey back after the fatigue of the ceremony and the accompanying banquet. They remained at the Adelphi, for the Bishop would never consent on such occasions to accept private hospitality. Indeed, the watchful wife began to fear she had done wrong in urging him to come at all; whatever was the reason, she said to herself, it was perfectly clear that Cecil could not bear to return to Liverpool.

In the evening, after dinner, they went into the comfortable drawing-room of the hotel; Mrs. Glisson fancied it might cheer Cecil up to have a little distracting. talk with the strangers he met there. An American liner had arrived that day; and among the guests were not a few of her passengers. The Bishop sat on a sofa trying to make conversation with one or two of these. Both parties, however, were distraught; the Bishop, by the events of that day of Purgatory; the Americans, by the novelty of the episcopal gaiters, and the strange apparition of the episcopal apron, both which they surveyed with irresistible amusement.

At last, one stranger strolled up and sat close by the Bishop. He was a solid-looking ruddy-haired man, with a farmer-like air, and when he spoke, the Bishop recognised at once the familiar Canadian accent of his boyhood. He had heard it twice or thrice during the intervening years; nay, more, he had even passed unrecognised among people whose names at least he had known at Brantford. But to-night, the coincidence was particularly distasteful to him. He was just about to say: " Olive, my dear, I think I shall go upstairs," when the new-comer leaned across and began conversation abruptly: " The Bishop of Dorchester, they tell me? "

The episcopal neck gave a faint inclination of assent.

" Well, you *were* Dr. Cecil Glisson, before you were made a bishop, I fancy," the stranger continued.

• Something vaguely familiar about the voice and face made the Bishop falter. " I was," he answered tremulously.

" Then you must have met my poor cousin Tom Pringle," the Canadian went on, unconscious of the bomb-shell he was so carelessly letting drop: " he sailed on the John Wesley."

The room swam round the Bishop. He grew white and red alternately. Olive came to the rescue at the very nick of time. " It was a most painful episode in my husband's life," she put in softly. " The memory of it never ceases to disturb him to this present day. It almost killed him. You know he was shot by the captain of the John Wesley; and he had been tenderly nursed, before the explosion, by your cousin, Tom Pringle."

" Oh, I know about all that," Hiram Pringle answered—for the Bishop now recognised his cousin after thirty-five years of absence. " I made lots of inquiries about poor Tom in Australia. He was blown up in the explosion, the same time that you were. Only, he didn't come to again. Well, Bishop, any way, I'm glad to meet you." He used the familiar Canadian mode of address which was the only one he knew. " I was fond of Tom, and I should like to hear from you anything you can tell me about the poor fellow's last voyage."

What was the Bishop to do? Under these trying circumstances, he could not seem cold and cruel toward the dead sailor who was supposed to have tended him carefully through a severe illness and probably to have died through his devotion to duty and his unwillingness to join Bully Ford and his comrades. In five minutes he found himself launching forth on a touching tribute to his own dead self; extolling his own tenderness, his care, his womanly nursing; making a hero and a martyr out of the very Tom Pringle who sat there that moment in a falsely-gained episcopal garb, hating himself inwardly for his own cowardice and deception. Tom Pringle—why the Tom Pringle who signed articles on the John Wesley was a moral innocent compared with the black heart of the Cecil Glisson who now wore his body.

The ruddy-haired man listened to him with real emotion. " Poor old Tom," he mused, with tears in his eyes, in spite of all the years; "he was a real good sort. Many's the time he and I played truant from school to go fishing for black bass and hunting mink in the creek—the creek down by Brantford—let me see, what did we call it?"

It was on the Bishop's tongue to answer "Little Cataraqui Creek," but he pulled himself up in time, and held a prudent silence.

"And you have prospered in this world, I suppose," he ventured to say at last, in his bland clerical voice, seeing that Hiram had the air of a man of money.

"Oh, pretty well," his cousin answered; "pretty well: I've made my pile: though you mustn't think, either, my cousin Tom was no more than a common seaman by birth because he was sailing as one when you happened to meet him. Tom was a better scholar than me, and a good-looking fellow, too: he might have been a gentleman if he hadn't chosen to run away to sea like a foolish young donkey. He had plenty of brains, Tom had. Yes, I've done pretty well for myself; gone into the lumber trade on the Upper Ottawa, and got tolerable concessions. I don't want to boast, but I ought to be worth to-day, say my million dollars."

"Two hundred thousand pounds!" the Bishop echoed, with perhaps more alacrity than was to be expected from a man who ought by his own account never to have set foot on the American continent. "That's a very large fortune. Well, perhaps your cousin Tom, if he had stopped in Canada, might have done as well in the end. There's no accounting for the wonderful dispensations of Providence."

"Though, mind you," Hiram interposed, "I think so well of Tom that I wouldn't think better of him not if he was wearing that pair of gaiters you have on this minute."

The Bishop reddened again; but fortunately Olive set his confusion down to what she considered an unsuitable allusion to the episcopal leggings.

Hiram scanned him from head to foot, with a slow long stare. "You're not unlike him either," he said. Then for a second a queer feeling came over him. He was just about to add slowly: "Why—you—are Tom Pringle"—when the absurdity of the identification burst upon him all at once, and he contented himself with saying: "You might be his brother."

The Bishop marked the look and the hesitating manner. He dared not risk it any longer.

"We were considered like one another on the John Wesley," he admitted stiffly. Then he rose and shook his cousin's hand. "Well, good night, Mr. Pringle," he went on, as cordially as he could manage. "I—I am glad to have met you." Oh, appalling falsehood! "I cannot fail to cherish the most friendly feelings towards any relation or friend of poor Tom Pringle, whom I remember with affection and gratitude and—and—Olive, my dear, give me your arm. I—I feel far from well. Mr Pringle must excuse me. And the sun was so hot! This day has been too much for me!"

Olive helped him to his room. He waved his hand to Hiram. Once safely upstairs, he broke down utterly. He sat on the side of the bed and cried like a baby. Olive blamed herself bitterly for bringing him there against his will. His nerves were out of gear. She decided she would never again urge him to take part in one of these horrid distasteful functions.

After all, she thought, he was quite right. She applied his own favourite test. The apostles never attended the laying of foundation stones with masonic honours.

But as he sat there that night, the Bishop made up his mind. This must cease for ever. He could not go on living this lie for a lifetime.

Each day that passed made the rôle more hateful. While he was a mere country parson, it had been easier to carry it off; but now, his very conspicuousness made his irksome task harder.

CHAPTER XXI

A QUESTION OF ORDINATION.

A WEEK or two later, there was a dinner party at the Palace; a clerical dinner party; what Evelyn irreverently described in her own curt dialect as "feeding the diocese." Evelyn was a "sport" in an episcopal family. Her language was based on the undergraduate model: her ideas were surreptitiously derived from yellow French romances.

Throughout the whole of dinner, Evelyn's manner had been uneasy. A Canon of Christ Church was among the guests, fresh over from the House. Evelyn asked him at dessert, having bottled up her eagerness so long with difficulty, whether the class-list in Greats was out yet. Oh, yes, out this afternoon, the Canon answered. Evelyn wondered, unconcernedly, who had got Firsts. "Two Christ Church men," the Canon believed. "I forget their names." Evelyn's anxiety controlled itself admirably.

That's the worst of a secret engagement, she thought to herself; you can't even have a telegram. Still, where would the fun of an engagement come in if it weren't secret? A girl who has the misfortune to belong to an episcopal household is hard put to it for romance; and Evelyn, for all her slanginess, was essentially romantic. The excitement of secrecy was worth to her mind even the consequent necessity for foregoing a telegram.

"Do you happen to remember whether Mr. Beddingley of Oriel got a Second?" she inquired in the same unconcerned tone. "He comes here sometimes."

"Why a Second, Evelyn?" the Bishop asked. "You prejudge the case, my child. It would have been kinder to ask whether he had got a First, wouldn't it?"

Evelyn shrugged her shoulders. "A faintly Second would be good bizz for poor little Beddingley," she answered.

"He's an excellent young man," Mrs. Glisson interposed, not even venturing to object to *bizz* as an element in a young lady's vocabulary. "He has such very high principles."

"I haven't measured them," Evelyn retorted, "so I don't know exactly how high they run; but if they're more than five feet five, they must stick up above his head, which would be uncomfortable for walking."

"My dear," her father interposed, "you are unjust to young Beddingley. He is precisely the sort of man I should choose by preference to assist me in the arduous work of a diocese."

"Cut out for an examining chaplain," Evelyn responded with a snap. "That's just how I measured him myself. He was born examining. But the Canon hasn't told us whether he got his Second."

"I forget whether his name was in the list," the Canon answered, pressing his lips together with a dubitative air, as when one judges an unknown vintage. "Beddingley; Beddingley; no," he shook his head; "I can't recall him."

"Then there was a Mr. Thornbury of Merton whom I met at the Dean's," Evelyn continued, with a carefully casual manner which Mrs. Glisson noted as a sure mark of much more active interest. "He was going in this term. Such a jolly young man. He won the hundred yards at the 'Varsity grinds. Do you happen to know whether he got a First?"

"Why not a Second?" Mrs. Glisson asked mischievously.

Evelyn betrayed herself by a faint blush.

" Because he's really clever," she answered,—
" and probably has principles several inches short-
er than Mr. Beddingley's. At least, he's six
inches taller; so perhaps on what Daddy calls
the law of compensation, he may make up in
height for what he lacks in principles. For my
own part, I prefer them to take it out that way.
I can never understand why people are so dead
stuck on principles." And she looked about her
defiantly.

" Thornbury? " the Canon repeated, rolling
the name on his palate, as one rolls an uncer-
tain port, to see whether he recognised it.
" Thornbury? Thornbury? Of Merton, did you
say? Yes, I *think* he got a Third; in fact, I recall
it now,—Thornbury of Merton."

But Evelyn was not looking or listening.
Suddenly her eyes had wandered at a bound
from the table and across the lawn; and had
fixed themselves on a fluttering white object that
flickered strangely above the green of the rhododendrons. She knew that sign well. It was
Alex Thornbury, creeping close in his canoe
under the garden bank, and giving her the signal
that he was there to meet her.

In a second, she had forgotten the strawber-
ries on her plate, and was full of the adventure.
Her own handkerchief fluttered unobtrusively

in reply. She must slip out somehow and learn from Alex himself whether or not he had really taken a Third in the Schools and thereby wrecked his chance of an inspectorship.

"What are you doing about Greenslade of Reading?" the Canon asked, changing the subject abruptly.

The Bishop's face grew dark. Two vertical lines marked his broad forehead. "Greenslade of Reading," he repeated. "Ah, it's a very sad business. One cannot help being grieved at it. It appears there can now be no shadow of doubt that the poor fellow was never ordained at all. His ordination letters have turned out on examination, I regret to say, to be a complete forgery."

"I'm sorry you've introduced the question, Canon," Mrs. Glisson broke in. "I've never known the Bishop so distressed and absorbed about anything since we came to Dorchester. It has been a terrible blow to him."

"He was such an excellent clergyman, you see," the Bishop continued. "Or rather, one thought him so. There was hardly a man in the diocese whom I respected and trusted more than I did poor Greenslade."

".It's a shocking disclosure," the Canon assented, helping himself to burnt almonds. "A most shocking disclosure. This is excellent Madeira."

"*The* interesting question to my mind," a country rector put in, " is this; how about the validity of the marriages he celebrated? "

Evelyn rose with sham dignity. "Oh, if you're going to discuss the validity of marriage," she observed in a mock serious voice, " this is no place for me. The episcopacy I can stand: episcopacy to-day is a social figment. But not the marriage question. I draw a line there. I think I had better go out into the garden." And she seized the opportunity.

Mrs. Glisson breathed freely.

" The marriages are valid," the Bishop went on, not heeding Evelyn's parenthesis. " That point has been decided for us already by the law courts. I have looked up the precedents and I find the case is fully provided for. A marriage is valid if solemnised in a church by the *de facto* incumbent, or by any person who has been accepted as a clergyman by the bishop of the diocese, and whom the parties involved have both regarded as a *bona fide* priest in holy orders of the Church of England."

" Yes; legally," the rector assented: he was a close-shaven person, thin-lipped, austere, with a very advanced cassock and a stiff white collar.

"That is a question for the law. But ecclesiastically and sacramentally? That's the point for *our* consideration. What I ask is this—*Can* the Church regard such persons as in any true sense married?"

The Bishop's lips were white. His voice faltered. "I cannot allow the word 'sacramentally' to pass without protest," he interposed, diverging to a side issue. "Marriage has never been admitted as a sacrament by the authoritative voice of the Church of England."

But the rector was not to be turned aside. "I waive that point," he said tartly; "though I do not allow that I unreservedly accept your lordship's correction. But, omitting the word sacrament, the important question for us as churchmen is this—a question for churchmen of all shades of opinion, sacramental or evangelical; are couples married by this man Greenslade, who was never a priest, or even a deacon, to be considered as married at all, in the Church's sense? or are they not rather to be regarded as living together in a legalised union, a meretricious union, in the same way as if they had merely been married, or rather united (for I cannot consent to call it marriage) by civil contract before a registrar?"

The Bishop paused. "It is a very grave

problem," he answered, with true episcopal caution, for a bishop must never give a categorical answer about anything on earth without reserving to himself some chance of hedging. "I would not care to decide it offhand without due deliberation."

"In *my* opinion," the rector observed with decision, "such couples are living in unconscious sin: they ought certainly to be remarried at once by an ordained clergyman. The bond in which they remain is a purely human one."

"I don't quite see that," the Canon interposed. He was a safe Moderate. "You are pushing the doctrine of priestly sanction one degree too far. Surely the children born already of such marriages are lawful children?"

"Lawful—yes—before the law; but born in Christian wedlock, no. The union, though unfortunate, is obviously not a Christian marriage. I would call such persons innocent but irregular."

The Bishop deliberated. His manner was distraught. "May we not say," he began, raising one didactic forefinger, "that here we must distinguish between the fact and the intention? The persons who unfortunately presented themselves to be married by our friend Greenslade—I mean, by this unhappy man who has so deeply disappointed our just expectations—presented themselves under the belief that they were being married by a *bona fide* priest of the Church of England. Their intention being thus ecclesiastically and formally correct, they are surely guiltless as laymen in the matter. Many of them may never chance to hear that Greenslade was not a priest at all; and such persons cannot, I should say, be considered as anything other than truly married. Charity, my dear sir, charity! Do not let us substitute an ecclesiastical figment for the plain fact that these people have conformed as far as they were able to the rules of the Church, and so have been as nearly married as they could manage. The intention, after all, is not the intention everything?"

But the rector was not to be silenced by mere episcopal opinion. His reverence for bishops was greater in the abstract than in the concrete—as often happens with members of his school of thought. "I do not say such people are living in open sin," he answered, bristling up. "That would be ignoring, as your lordship suggests, their innocence in intention. Or rather, I would put it, they are living in sin, but with innocent ignorance of the fact; and to commit a sinful act not knowing that you commit it leaves the nature of the act in itself unchanged, though it may of course excuse the person. I would not assert that such people are actually doing wrong; but I do assert that the moment they discover the true state of the case, it becomes their bounden duty as members of the Church to put themselves right by getting remarried at once—or, to speak more correctly, by substituting a regular and canonical marriage for the irregular and really impious ceremony in which they have unwittingly and unwillingly taken part."

"It would no doubt be safer," the Canon admitted. He preferred constitutionally to be on the safe side.

"Put it this way," the rector went on, warming up to his subject. "Suppose, for argument's sake, a person understood to be a bishop, and acting as such, were found some day to be in reality a pretender——"

"WHAT?" the Bishop exclaimed, giving a sudden start from his chair and turning white with emotion. "A bishop in forged orders!"

"I put the case *argumenti gratia*, my lord," the rector went on, still blandly, though taken aback by the startled way his diocesan received this appalling suggestion. "If it is permitted by Providence that a simple priest should deceive the faithful, it might surely be permitted that a bishop should do likewise. Indeed I believe it is historically true that just as there have been antipopes, there have been antiepiscopi. Now, do you mean to assert that the persons ordained, or apparently ordained, by such a mock bishop, are really priests in any ecclesiastical sense? Could such persons for a moment be permitted to administer the sacraments of the Church for instance?"

"Certainly not," the Canon answered.

But the Bishop said nothing. It was not the rector's argument that silenced him. He leant back in his chair, very deeply perturbed. He had tried for years to keep from asking himself these very questions, and now he could delay them no longer. This case of Mr. Greenslade had made a solution of the point imperative. Do what he would, there was no way out of it. He must face the question from the ecclesiastical point of view; what enormity had he committed by pretending to be a bishop when he was not even a priest? and what was the status of the priests and deacons ordained by him, and all the persons admitted by him to confirmation and other rites of the Church?

Lost in his own reverie, the Bishop leaned back in his place and let the stream of dialectics flow by him unperceived, while the Canon, the rector, and the other clergymen at table took sides either way as to the validity of acts performed by one who was not a priest but supposed to be so.

"If such an interloper were never discovered," the Canon objected, "he might even become a bishop; and in that case, apostolic succession might altogether be vitiated."

"The Welsh and Cornish clergy of the old Celtic Church were not lawfully consecrated," another disputant objected. "It is doubtful, according to the latest authorities, whether they were even priests. They were certainly not bishops. The way in which they received the apostolic succession, if any, is far from certain. They were undoubtedly heretics. The way in which they conformed is still unknown; and we cannot discover whether they were ever really reconciled to the Church, and admitted to orders, or whether their status was irregularly recognised by the See of Canterbury. So that the whole of the Church in Wales and Cornwall may suffer from the very irregularity you mention."

"And that irregularity," the Canon continued, "must have affected the entire body of the Church of England; for priests ordained by Welsh and Cornish Britons may have risen in time to be English bishops."

"More than that," said the historian of the

party. " For since Nicholas Breakspear, who became pope as Adrian IV., was ordained in the West Country, he had probably some taint of these irregular Celtic orders; and that taint, he, as pope, may have imported into universal Latin Christendom."

The Bishop caught that last phrase and gave a sigh of relief. After all, he was not the only man through whom offences had come; though he knew it was better that a millstone should be tied round his neck and he should be cast into the sea than that he should thus vitiate the whole stream of the Church of England.

CHAPTER XXII.

A LIGHTER TREATMENT.

Meanwhile, Evelyn had slipped from the table half unperceived, and strolled down with ostentatious carelessness to the weeping willow by the water's edge.

She did not get into her canoe at once, however, though the boat-house lay close beside the willow. To have done so, before her mother's eyes, and in her light evening dress, would have been to court enquiry, if not prohibition. So she wandered about aimlessly among the rhododendron beds, instead, picking a white pink now and again and smelling at it ostentatiously, as if she were merely engaged in walking around to cool herself after the heat of the dining-room and the theological discussion. Thence, by slow degrees, she disappeared behind the rose-bushes, and gradually worked her way back again unperceived to the boat-house. There, she slipped in quietly, while Mrs. Glisson's eyes were fixed with mute attention on the silent white face of the Bishop; and, seating herself in her canoe, pushed it out under the bank, bending low as she did so lest her mother should perceive her. In two minutes more, she was safe behind the loose-strife, and paddling at all speed for Day's Lock and the backwater.

A second canoe awaited her among the irises. Evelyn paddled up with rapid strokes till she was within talking distance. "Well?" she called out in haste, and in a very eager voice. "A First? Now wasn't it?"

Alex nodded in reply. "Yes, a First," he answered gaily. "They say, the best First of the year." And he laughed aloud in his triumph.

Evelyn affected not to be relieved, though the Canon's false report had really alarmed her. "I knew it," she answered carelessly. "I hadn't the slightest fear, dear old man, that you wouldn't get one." But she showed her relief in her face, for all that; and she permitted herself to be kissed with a tender yielding which was not quite her wont. As a rule, she pretended that demonstrations of affection were detrimental to her bodice, her hair, or her laces. "Maud took the kiss sedately," says Tennyson. A lady should take it so. But Evelyn did not always rise to this standard of taste; she was apt to

make believe she did not care about kissing—
a pretence more common at a lower level.

She withdrew her face, flushed. "Then, in
that case," she said slowly, "it occurs to me,
we are engaged, Alex."

"I believe so," Alex answered, still clinging
to her hand. "You said you wouldn't be engaged to me till I had got through my Schools.
Though what precise difference being engaged
makes to us I don't quite know, Evey. It seems
to be a purely grammatical distinction. I never
could understand it."

"I think," Evelyn answered, "it makes this
difference—that we look forward to getting married, more or less, some time or other."

"Oh, that's it, is it?" Alex asked, seizing
her hand once more.

Evelyn nodded her head sagely. "So I've
always understood," she answered.

"But meanwhile, Evey—I may?"

"Yes, if you like, Alex. . . . There, that's
quite enough now. Suppose somebody were to
come, dear."

"Nobody'll come."

"Well, they're all in the dining-room at present, discussing the validity of orders or something. Mums is looking after Daddy. He's
got apostolical succession awfully bad on the

brain this evening. So I expect we're all right. Apostolical succession is always a safe draw for an hour's discussion. . . . Well, the next thing is, we must see about this inspectorship."

"I might get a fellowship, Evey, if it weren't for——"

"No, you'd never get a fellowship, dear boy. I've asked one or two men—dons, don't you know; and they told me that was out of the question, because of screwing up the Tutor. I know it was all right; but they say it wouldn't do as a matter of discipline. The episode was too public. So you must try the inspectorship."

"Even then, we couldn't marry, I'm afraid, for ever and ever so long."

"I don't care. If only we're engaged. Being engaged is nice enough. It's rather a mistake being in such a precious hurry to get married. Men are always like that. I believe most girls prefer a tolerably long engagement. Just tolerably long, don't you know; not quite as long as the face you're making; but just about *so* long. It gives one time to roll about the fact of being engaged on one's palate. One gets the taste of it so. You men want to bolt it. You're always so greedy."

"How can one help it, Evey, when you look so sweetly saucy?"

"Well, *that's* not business. I'm ever so glad you've got this First though, Alex: but I always knew you'd get it. Didn't I say so when you told me you hadn't read all last term? I said: 'Oh, nonsense; you're clever enough to do it on your own, if you choose, without reading.' And you were, you see. So I was right. There are men, like Mr. Beddingley, who can mug and grub and just manage to scrape through with a Third, after reading for ages; and there are men like you who can pull through without trying, and get a First into the bargain. By the bye, where did poor little Beddingley come out?"

"A Third."

"I told you so! Mums *will* be angry. She has destined me in her own mind for poor dear little Beddingley. She's gone on that man: he has 'such very high principles!' She means him to be Daddy's examining chaplain; and me to marry him; and she intends to push him into a minor canonry; and so, through the regular gradation, till he's a prebendary or something. He's so thoroughly mediocre that he's sure to succeed. Don't you fancy me married to a prebendary, Alex! I wonder what prebendaries are supposed to do. It's a worse puzzle than arch-deacons. And I look as if I were cut out for one!"

She held her paddle at an angle which indicated the expectation of an immediate advance from the opposite side. Alex accepted the hint. "You wicked little pagan, you look like the sauciest, naughtiest little girl that ever disgraced an episcopal palace," he answered, leaning over and kissing her. "Evey, it's all too delightful, to-night. I've got my First; and I've got you with me; and I'm going to marry you; and I won't go home to Oxford till I don't know what hour; and as for the proctor, I don't care a——"

"Oh, hush; naughty boy;" she clapped her hand on his mouth. "And in the Palace grounds too! If Mums were to hear you she'd—— Now, Alex, take care! you'll really upset me."

So they continued to discuss the possibilities of an inspectorship, and the probable length of their engagement—Evelyn's preference for length growing restrained each time to more and more modest limits—while the party in the dining-room were occupied at the same time in discussing the validity of early Celtic orders. Mrs. Glisson's eyes were fixed hard upon the Bishop. His look was vacant. More than ever she feared the strain of the diocese was telling upon him. So deeply intent was she upon her husband that she almost forgot for the time her watchful care of her daughter. And indeed, in that party, she had no reason to fear for Evelyn; though Evelyn, she admitted to herself, was the sort of girl who could get into mischief whenever one turned one's back; but what harm could a girl, with the best intentions of mischief, manage to extract from the rhododendron beds at the Palace or the dear old Canon? And Cecil this evening was more distraught than ever; she feared the double care of the diocese and of his weight of learning was beginning to tell even upon that fine physique which he had brought from Australia.

So for an hour or two she never thought more of Evelyn. After coffee had been served, however, and the details of the Wallingford Ruridecanal Association discussed at full, it suddenly occurred to her that Evelyn was still missing. Could she have gone out in the canoe—in her thin evening dress—and at this hour of the evening? and if so, could she have managed to upset herself and get into the river? Visions of Evelyn drowned rose vivid before her maternal eyes. Yet even in her momentary dread, she would not unnecessarily disturb or frighten dear Cecil. He had more than enough burdens of his own already. She would stroll out into the grounds and look herself for Evelyn.

She walked along the bank as far as the boathouse. It was even as she feared. The canoe was missing! If nothing worse had happened, the child would catch her death of cold in that light Roumanian embroidered muslin blouse, and not even a shawl to throw over her shoulders. Much alarmed for Evelyn's safety, she continued her way along the water's edge, till she had reached the backwater. There, a confused murmur of voices struck her ear, coming from a thick bed of wild yellow irises. Mrs. Glisson paused. Her first feeling was one of sincere thankfulness. Evelyn was not drowned, at any rate; that was her voice, for one. But the other—was a man's. And what man could Evelyn have picked up with at Dorchester?

Maternal solicitude made Mrs. Glisson risk a wetting of her feet. She stepped down on to a knoll of tufted sedge among the irises. Then she craned her neck and looked over softly.

An alarming vision burst upon her eyes. Evelyn and a man whom she did not even know by sight were bidding one another an affectionate adieu, with the usual demonstrations of their age and relation.

Mrs. Glisson was taken aback. "Evelyn," she called out severely, "is that you?"

"Yes, Mums," the Bishopina answered, unmoved, taking the bull by the horns. "And this is Mr. Thornbury. Alex, dear, my mother." ·

Mrs. Glisson gasped. "But, my child, you are out here—at this hour—in that very thin frock—and alone!"

"No, Mamma; not alone; with Mr. Thornbury."

"But—we do not know him!"

"Oh, that doesn't matter, Mums; it's all right. *He's* Alex. There's no harm in that. You see, I'm engaged to him."

For a moment Mrs. Glisson was inclined to be miserable. Then it recurred to her at once that she too had been a girl; and that she too had got engaged to dear Cecil without the parental sanction. Though to be sure, that was to *Cecil*—while this was only to some unknown person. Still, she recognised at once that Evelyn was a very peculiar girl, who would have her own way, and to give Evelyn her way was the only safe course with her. So she made up her mind at once. "In that case," she said promptly, with unexpected acquiescence, "I think Mr. Thornbury had better step up to the house and see your Papa, and we can put things at once on a regular basis."

Alex stood up in his canoe, with his hat in his hand, looking peculiarly sheepish. A man always finds such positions trying. But Evelyn was quite unabashed. "Very well, dear," she answered. "That's just as you wish. Sooner or later, I suppose, we *must* tell Daddy about it. And the betting is always five to one on sooner against later. Alex is at Merton, Mums, and he was just going to catch the last train to Oxford when you came and interrupted us. I expect now you've made him lose it. So he'll have to sleep at the Palace all night, and Daddy'll have to write and tell his Tutor he was delayed with us by accident."

She said it with gusto; for this sort of adventure exactly suited her.

CHAPTER XXIII.

AN OFFICIAL INTERVIEW.

"Sir Nathaniel will see you at once," said the Private Secretary, in the most deferential of his twenty-seven carefully graduated manners. "But he hopes your business will be brief, my lord: for he expects a deputation from the Congregationalists and Baptists at 11.30; in spite of which, he would really *like* to give you a few minutes. This way, if you please. Lovely morning, isn't it?"

The Bishop followed the underling into the great man's inner room. Sir Nathaniel Merriton raised his head from a pile of papers, which he thrust away wearily. "Ah, Dr. Glisson?" he said in his big languid voice, as of a tired giant. "Delighted to see you, my dear bishop. I don't think we've met since you've worn a mitre. *Do* you wear a mitre, by the way? Dr. Gregory of Lindisfarne was at Oxford with me, you know, and in those day had hardly more theology, I'm afraid, than the rest of us. He preferred Catullus to the Pauline Epistles. But I went down to Northumberland a few weeks since—on official business, I need hardly say—I am the slave of the office; and whom should I see at a function in the Minister, but Charlie Gregory, if you please, as my Lord Bishop *in excelsis*, wearing a pea-green object on his back which I should describe in my ignorance as probably a cope, and carrying in his hands what I should also be inclined (under correction) to designate as a crozier. It was awfully funny. And I remember when Charlie Gregory lighted a fire in Tom-Quad, and was promptly sent down for it."

"A man outlives such things," the Bishop said wearily. (He does *not* outlive being a wolf in sheep's clothing.)

"Some people do—and some people don't," the representative of governmental education replied with cheerful tolerance. "It's the old story, you know; one man may steal a horse, and another mayn't look over the hedge. That's popular wisdom. We have it exemplified here. *You* are the only bishop on the bench I would have received this morning. Very undiplomatic to tell you so, you think. Not at all; not at all: most diplomatic. For does not true diplomacy consist in knowing and understanding your man? If I had said that to the Bishop of Lindisfarne, for example, he would have commented upon it at a Church Congress as a gross slight to the episcopate. But when I say it to *you*, I know that you will accept it as a personal compliment to the most reasonable and. moderate bishop on the bench. So, having greased the wheels of conversation with a little judicious compliment, let's get to business. I'm expecting these interminable Baptists at half past eleven. I call them interminable to *you* in strict confidence. Believe me, my dear sir, Baptists are almost as exacting as bishops; and between the two, the upper and nether grindstones of the educational mill, you behold me crushed—annihilated."

Sir Nathaniel drew himself up to his six feet four, with shoulders to match, and looked about as little crushed as any man in England. But the Bishop understood him. What he said was true. He could talk the usual circumlocutory dialect of Government offices whenever that tongue was necessary; but he could also unbend when he chose with a very effective candour which committed him to nothing, while it flattered his companion with a sense of belonging to the inner circle.

The Bishop discussed for ten minutes or so the affairs of the Church schools in the diocese of Dorchester, which were the object of his visit.

Sir Nathaniel listened; assented; stifled a yawn; smiled genially; was cordial in generalities, and when it came to particulars would give his best consideration (but no immediate answer) to all practical suggestions the Bishop had to urge upon him. He was suave and non-committing. "By the way," he said at last, turning over some papers listlessly, "there will be a vacancy, I see, for a junior examiner in your district by Christmas. It is strictly irregular; but I ask between ourselves. I ask for information merely; it being my duty to make things as comfortable as I can for all parties concerned, without, if I may be excused the expression, making hay of the public service. Now, *is* there any candidate or any existing inspector whom you would particularly like to see transferred to your circuit? Because, if so, we make it a rule *never* to be influenced in the slightest degree by the private wishes of anybody and more especially of bishops; but we *might* consider the person in the ordinary rotation; and *if* he happened to be in all respects by far the most suitable public servant we could find for the place, and *if* we felt disposed to risk appointing him, the fact that you desired to have him there at your side, might possibly not be allowed to tell against him. I say, it might possibly not; and on the other hand it might possibly be fatal to his chances. Government is government. So if you care to hazard it, and will mention anyone, this department will endeavour to forget the person's name at once, and will appoint entirely in the public interest."

"I understand that, of course," the Bishop answered in his guileless way. "And I shall not be surprised if I find my candidate is not appointed."

"Nor if you find he is," Sir Nathaniel interposed, smiling. "We are impartial, recollect, im-partial. These things cut both ways."

"Oh, certainly," the Bishop said, smiling in turn, he knew not why.

"Well, what name?" the Secretary went on, glancing aside at the clock.

"His name?" the Bishop answered; "oh, his name—I forgot—is Alexander Thornbury. He has just taken his degree—First in Greats—at Oxford. His college—Merton. And I ought to inform you at once, lest I should seem to hold back the fact at the outset, that he has got himself engaged, without my consent, to my daughter Evelyn."

The great man laughed. "But has obtained that consent *ex post facto?*" he chimed in.

"That is about the true state of the case, Sir Nathaniel."

"Well, so far as it goes, that circumstance does not seem to tell against him. If you are prepared to entrust him with your daughter's happiness, *ex post facto* or otherwise, you have probably confidence in his abilities and his honour."

"At any rate, Evelyn has," the Bishop responded with the parental dutifulness of the nineteenth century.

"Miss Evelyn is a young lady of great discrimination," the Secretary observed.

"I trust so," the Bishop assented.

Sir Nathaniel reflected. "His name is down?" he queried at last.

"Yes; but only since a week ago."

"Well, *if* this department were going to appoint him at all," the Secretary continued, in an abstracted voice, "it had better be soon. Delay is dangerous. Is the engagement announced?"

"No," the guileless Bishop answered promptly. "But why?"

Sir Nathaniel stroked his chin and looked across at his caller with a comical air of amusement. "Well," he answered slowly, "if I were you, I would *not* announce it,—till after some-

body or other has been appointed to this vacancy.
We must avoid a job. Whoever happens to be
appointed, it would be quite in the natural course
of events that your daughter should thereafter
by chance be thrown in with him, and proceed
to fall in love with him, or he with her, which-
ever is the fashionable phrase of the moment.
Therefore, I advise your daughter to wait—I am
speaking unofficially, without involving the department—and only to get herself engaged to
whatever person we may happen to appoint, *after*
we have appointed him. If we were to do anything else, don't you see, there might be a suspicion of jobbery."

"But my dear sir," the Bishop cried, warming up, "you know Evelyn; and you don't mean
to say you suppose she is the sort of girl who
could fall in love to order with whatever young
man you may happen to send us!"

Sir Nathaniel gazed down at him through his
pince-nez with a pitying smile, as one might gaze
at a specimen of a rare and interesting but almost
extinct animal. "My dear Bishop," he said at
last, fingering the ends of his moustache, "you
do *not* understand official language yet;—and it's
my belief you never will, either. You are a very
difficult man to whom to do a service. Here am
I positively putting myself into a position that

might endanger the administration all through my personal feeling of liking for yourself—giving away the show, so to speak—creating a possible public scandal—and telling you so as plainly as a public servant can dare to tell it in these degenerate days—all because I consider a recommendation from you worth ten reams at least of ordinary testimonials; and you refuse to understand! Oh, you unsophisticated person! Please go away and inform everybody but Miss Glisson how I assured you—as I do now assure you—that nothing save merit on the part of the candidate can ever be taken into consideration by this department; and tell Miss Glisson that I send her my kindest regards—my *very* kindest regards—it used to be 'love' and 'Evelyn,' I recollect, when she was smaller—and that only a sense of public duty prevents my being able to make the slightest concession in favour of any candidate in whom she happens to be interested. But a sense of public duty renders it quite impossible for me. *She* will understand, if you don't. She's a sensible girl, and she knows what a man means when he tells her his intentions in painfully plain and most unofficial language."

" I'll write your message down, I think," the Bishop said, taking out his note-book. " You said, ' Tell Miss Glisson——' "

"Oh no, you won't!" Sir Nathaniel answered, with an uncontrollable fit of laughter, seizing his hand and pencil. "Put up that note-book! I'm not going to let you say you took down my very words, my *ipsissima verba*, in writing. This is a private and wholly unofficial interview. I will shorten my message and spare your memory. Tell your daughter that if she looks in the Times daily for the next six weeks she will find out whether or not her *protégé* is appointed. Remark that I say *protégé*. Bear that word in mind. For, if you venture to say *fiancé*,—you upset the government."

The Bishop returned to Dorchester bewildered; officialdom was one of those things he could *not* understand, though he had written a book on the Comparative Grammar of the Melanesian Languages. But when he told Evelyn, word for word, as far as he was able to remember, what the Education Office had said, she laughed and kissed him, and answered: "There's a dear old Dad; Alex has got the appointment!" And though the Bishop couldn't for the life of him make out how Evelyn knew, he was sure she was right; and he was relieved when she added: "But I won't mention it to anybody, and we'll keep the engagement dark; and when next I see Sir Nathaniel I shall set his mind at rest by telling him I'm determined *not* to wreck so admirable a Government."

These things are hidden from the wise and prudent, the Bishop thought, and revealed (in our days) to babes and sucklings!

CHAPTER XXIV.

"Well, good bye, Evey; it's dreadful to say good bye; but there's no way out of it. I can't stop at Oxford after all the men have gone down; and I've got no money to go to London and live, as I should like to, running down here twice a week. So I must just go home till work turns up somewhere."

Parting made Evelyn almost old-fashioned in her tenderness. "It's so far, Northumberland," she said wistfully. "I do wish it was nearer. But I shall write to you every day, Alex; and it won't be so *very* long. Oh, I can't think why your people go and bury themselves in Northumberland!"

"Nor can I. It's out of the world. You can't get from there anywhere. But beggars and parsons can't be choosers."

"People ought to be able to live where they d. p.," Evelyn exclaimed with emphasis,—the depth of her emotion almost justifying her mitigated profanity. "And a country rectory, too! I know the horrid holes. There's one comfort, anyhow—you'll have lots of time for writing to me."

"Oh, won't I just! Evey, I'll write you such letters—as long as that. And I'll leave no stone unturned to get work immediately."

"Oh, as to work, I'm not a bit afraid. Sir Nathaniel says positively you shall have the first appointment he can find to give you."

"But your father told me just the opposite; he said Sir Nathaniel assured him it was impossible nowadays to make interest with government departments, and that nothing but merit could be considered in filling up public appointments."

"You silly boy! you're just as bad as Daddy! How innocent you men are! Isn't it precisely the same thing? What was language made for?"

"To say, 'What a darling you are, Evey!' And lips were made to kiss you with. When you call me a silly boy, I always feel it's the highest compliment. Isn't it funny to think that thousands and thousands of lovers have said just the same things to one another in their time as you and I say now? and yet, you and I are never tired of saying them."

" I don't think they can have said *quite* such nice things," Evelyn faltered, with a mist in her eyes.

" Just the very same, I'm told; but, Evey, they couldn't have *felt* them as you and I feel them!"

" Oh, dear no," Evelyn cried, clenching her little fists hard. " Fancy Daddy and Mums ever having talked like this—or held hands as we do. But people were different in those days, I suppose. And yet, I don't quite know; for Romeo and Juliet was written ever and ever so long ago; I was reading it last night:—and Romeo and Juliet talk much the same as we do."

" That's rather a compliment to us, Evey, isn't it? "

" Rude boy; you shouldn't say so."

" Another for that. Thank you. Well, I wish I was sure Sir Nathaniel really meant it. But your father gave me quite the opposite impression. And it was your father who saw him."

" But he's *written* to me," Evelyn cried. " Look here; this is his letter. He couldn't speak plainer! "

Alex took it and read—

" MY DEAR MISS GLISSON: (It was ' Evey ' once. Ah, these cruel years; how they rob us of everything!) Well, I am sorry to have to write and disappoint you. Your father tells me there is a young Oxford man (I forget his name) whom you desire to see appointed to an inspectorship in your district. Now, if I were not a government servant, I should hasten at once to oblige a lady. Unfortunately, however, placed as I am, it is impossible for me, consistently with the rules of the service, to exert any personal influence in favour of any particular candidate. Appointments are made by the department *entirely by merit*. No doubt, your protégé *has* merit; and *if* so, his chances will be as good as anyone else's. But not otherwise. Government is government.

"We hope to be on the river shortly, when my wife promises herself the pleasure of bringing the electric launch round to Dorchester, and will ask you to go for a few picnics with us. Meanwhile, I am, with—it *used* to be, love,

"Yours most sincerely,

"NATHANIEL MERRITON."

Alex scanned it dubiously. "Well, I can't say," he said in a disappointed tone, "I see anything in it of the nature of a promise."

"Oh, you ineffable goose!" Evelyn exclaimed. "What *could* he say plainer, unless he wrote 'I will make a job of it and appoint your man, if he's as ignorant as a turkey-cock '? Though why turkey-cocks should be more ignorant than any other birds I haven't the faintest conception. But look here—he underlines ' entirely by merit.' And he says, ' no doubt your protégé *has* merit; *if* so—' What could be clearer than that—without absolutely rendering himself liable to be sent to the Tower, or whatever else they do nowadays with wicked ministers? And then he puts: ' It was *Evvy* once.' And he goes out of his way to tell me Lady Merriton will call with the electric launch. Why, he's a dear, Sir Nathaniel! If I had him here this minute, I do declare, I'd just throw my arms right round his neck and kiss him! "

"In that case, I have no reason to regret his absence."

" There you are with your horrid little sneering Oxford epigrams. I know that style, sir. Little Beddingley can talk like that. But, Alex, you're going away; so I'll forgive you anything."

" And you're sure he'll appoint me? "

" Sure? A gun isn't in it. I know he means it. Before Christmas, too. And then, Alex——" She nestled up to him.

" You women are not in such a hurry, you know," Alex put in maliciously. " You *prefer* long engagements! "

"I said 'moderately long.' And then, you weren't going away. Just think, I shan't see you, perhaps, till Christmas! But I shall write to you every day. Oh, dear, oh dear; Dorchester will seem so unfurnished without you!"

"Well, good bye, Evey. I think we ought to say good bye now. I *must* catch that last train; and I have to take an official farewell of your mother in the drawing-room. She's been awfully good, as mothers go, to let us have such a nice long time out here alone together. Mothers never *were* young, you see; they don't know how we long to be left to ourselves. But she's good, as mothers go. I *must* go back to her."

"Good bye, darling; good bye! You *are* such a dear. I wish you *weren't* such a dear; I wish I'd taken little Beddingley—for I could say good bye to him for ever and never mind it. But *you*, Alex,—oh dear, I don't know how I'm ever to get on for six months, six whole months without you!"

CHAPTER XXV.

THE CLOUDS THICKEN.

ALL that evening, the Bishop sat close in his study. He was consulting books—books, books, books, innumerable. It was a question of conscience he was engaged in resolving. And how resolve it? What reparation could a man make for such a sin as *he* had committed?

For years he had shirked it; now, he could shirk it no longer. He must escape at last from this false position in the best way possible.

His first idea was to make reparation for his wrong by bringing down upon himself some fitting punishment. Suppose, for example, he were to forge a cheque in such a way that it was certain of detection? Then he would doubtless be tried, found guilty, and duly imprisoned. But, what difficulties in the way! In the first place, if the signature was obviously false, all the world would merely say poor Dr. Glisson had gone mad; and instead of punishing him, they would pack him off to a comfortable private asylum,

with all the consideration his age and rank suggested. Or, even if he succeeded, he would be
punished, not for the wrong he had really done,
but for a wrong he had only formally and peni-
tentially committed. No, the cheque was useless. It shirked the real difficulty. He must in
some way atone for his own actual crime; and
the only true atonement implied confession.

Confession! There was the horror. He could
have borne it for himself; but Olive, Olive!
How could he ever let her know that all his life
with her, all his life since the very first day he
met her, was a deception and a falsehood—that
he was not Cecil Glisson but Tom Pringle the
sailor—that he had never been a clergyman—
that everything she believed about him was lies,
lies, lies, from the very beginning? All the rest
of the world counted for nothing to him now;
but to let Olive know that the man she had
loved, believed in, trusted never existed at all
—oh, it was more than he could even endure to
think of.

And behind this dread of disillusionment for
Olive rose another terrible spectre which he
feared to look upon. A professional spectre. He
was not, he had never been, a priest at all. Yet
you cannot live for thirty years as a priest, you
cannot hold the cure of souls and rise to be a

bishop, without growing by degrees thoroughly ecclesiastical in your. ideas and feelings. Tom Pringle, Cecil Glisson, whatever he called himself—for even to himself he had half forgotten by this time his own original name—was now in all essentials, save the spiritual ones recognised by high sacerdotalists, an Anglican bishop. He thought and felt and saw things bishop-wise. And his terrible responsibility came home to him that night with a bishop's acquired professional sentiment. He magnified his office—the office that was not and had never been his; he knew he had been instrumental in ordaining false priests who thought themselves true ones; in marrying couples who in the eyes of the Church were never married; in upsetting in a thousand ways the organisation of Christianity in his various parishes and his present diocese. His offence was rank. He was an interloper and a fraud; he had caused many men to sin unwittingly; he had polluted and distorted the true stream of the means of grace; his guilt before heaven was great and unutterable. He was not even sure that he had not committed that unforgivable sin on which he had preached in his time more than one eloquent sermon. He stood abased before his God, a self-convicted offender.

Yet deep as was his sense of that ecclesi-

astical wrong, his feeling of shame before Olive
was profounder even now than his consciousness
of wrong before the eyes of the Almighty. Omniscience knew always the full extent of his
criminality; Olive did not. Omniscience could
allow for the chain of accident; but how confess
to Olive the long-continued deception?

Indeed, in his heart of hearts, it was not the
sense of sin at all that oppressed the Bishop; it
was the sense of a deep wrong done to others.
Like all greater natures, when brought face to
face with the consequences of their acts, 'twas
not forgiveness for himself that he asked, but
some chance of making reparation to others,
some loophole of escape from the injustice he
was doing them. If he broke Olive's heart, what
mattered forgiveness? if he caused others to go
astray, what could personal repentance avail to
repair that evil? Nay rather, would it not comfort him to hide his head in nethermost hell that
night if only so he could undo the harm he had
done to his innocent Olive?

All night long, he tossed and turned on his
bed, unable to sleep, unable to dismiss this appalling torment. He stood at the parting of two
impossible ways. He could no longer go on as
he had been going for years; he could not yet
turn aside and own the truth to Olive.

Early next morning, distracted with doubt, before the first cart rumbled over the bridge, he rose and dressed himself. He eat no breakfast, —in his present fierce mood it was a sort of cold comfort to him to mortify the flesh—but started on foot for the railway station, whence he took the first train of the day to Oxford.

Dr. Littlemore of Oriel was a saintly man— the last survivor of the famous group which had included Newman, Pusey, and Keble. To Dr. Littlemore he would go, then, and lay before him, under the seal of confession, this difficult question.

He arrived, all breathless, at the gates of Oriel. It was still early in the day, and the doctor had not breakfasted. His servant doubted whether he could yet see anyone. But the Bishop was urgent. This was a question of discipline; could Dr. Littlemore give him an interview immediately?

He was ushered into a formal oak-panelled study. Presently, the great casuist crept in,— a little white-haired, ferret-faced man, thin, spare, and bent, with ascetic features, and keen grey eyes that even in age had not lost their sharpness. He shook the Bishop's hot hand. Full of fierce emotion, the Bishop fell on his knees at once before the great confessor, and asked whether the father would receive a confession, treating it, whatever came, as sacrosanct and inviolable?

Dr. Littlemore, with a fox-like smile, answered at once and unhesitatingly: " Yes,—if it were murder."

" But if it were a sin against the Church—a sin against the Holy Ghost?" the Bishop cried, with his livid white face uplifted. " A sin that may have caused many to go astray? Would you keep it secret still, under the seal of confession? "

The confessor hesitated. " If it were something the suppression of which entailed danger to souls," he answered slowly—" I hardly know as yet: give me time to consider. The point is one which has not practically occurred to me." He suspected that unbelief had overcome the Bishop.

" I cannot give time," the Bishop answered, trembling with anxiety. " I must have an answer *now*. Will you hear me, and keep my secret? "

" I will," Dr. Littlemore replied after a short pause for thought. " It is best to hear. A man in your position in the Church would not come to me thus were it not for some grave and urgent reason."

The Bishop knelt before him like a little child, in a fervour of repentance, and poured forth in one wild flood the whole story of the secret that he had caged in his own breast for so many years of gnawing silence. He told all, without the slightest attempt at palliation or self-vindication. He explained the whole suite of accidents that led to the deception, indeed: but the deception itself he acknowledged without reserve or excuse. He made things if anything rather worse than they were instead of making them better. A fever of penitence and self-abasement was upon him. He longed to utter the whole truth, to have it out for once, to gain a moment's sympathy, or if not sympathy at least a hearing, from some fellow-creature.

The one person to whom under any other circumstances he would have poured forth everything was naturally Olive; and Olive was now the one person on earth to whom it was most impossible he should let out one word of it.

Dr. Littlemore listened with an awed and horrified face. The shock was unutterable. To the tremulous old priest, this was the worst crime the heart of man could conceive, a sin of the deepest blackness against the majesty of heaven. More than that, it was a sin the far-reaching consequences of which were beyond calculation. Theft and murder were nothing to it. It was a conspiracy against souls. Men and women were living in unblessed unions, unconsecrated hands were dispensing the sacramental mysteries, endless confusion had crept into the divine order of things, all because this one man had rashly dared to constitute himself what only the organised voice of the divine Church itself could suffice to make him. He had sinned the sin of Korah, Dathan, and Abiram. Dr. Littlemore almost waited to see earth open wide and swallow him up visibly as it swallowed up the pretenders to the office of Aaron.

At the end, he shut his eyes and remained long silent. Words failed his emotion. The Bishop bent his awed head and awaited judgment.

" The first question for me," the casuist said at last, speaking slowly and deliberately, with deep suppressed feeling, " is, ought I to have promised to keep your secret? Shall I do right in allowing a man who is not even a priest to continue fulfilling episcopal functions? "

The Bishop brushed away that question with one conclusive phrase. " Whatever comes, I am done with all that; I will never again act either as priest or as bishop."

" Even so," the old man faltered, his lips too

grown white, "am I doing my duty by the Church of God in concealing the fact of such grave irregularities?"

The Bishop bowed his head. "That is for you," he said, "to answer, Father."

They sat long in counsel. Dr. Littlemore prayed, exhorted, deliberated. But slowly the Bishop began to perceive that they two were attacking opposite problems. The casuist was thinking mainly of how he could save this erring soul by confession and repentance. The Bishop cared nothing for his individual soul—his soul might answer for its wrong-doing, and welcome, if only he could save Olive from that terrible dis-illusion. It was not eternal torment for him-self he dreaded; he could welcome eternal tor-ment like many other brave men; but a moment of fierce suffering, of incredible horror for the woman he had loved and deceived and wor-shipped was more than he could face: his whole soul shrank from it.

"I cannot tell my wife," he cried; "I cannot tell my wife! What becomes of myself, here or hereafter, I care very little; let Heaven punish my sin: but I must shield my dear wife—I must shield her at all hazards."

Dr. Littlemore was shocked. In his narrower creed, a man's first duty was to save his own soul, and after his own, the souls of others. That a person in a fever of repentance should wholly disregard his own future welfare seemed to him incredible. But the Bishop was built on broader lines. " Let my soul burn for ever, in burning hell, if such atonement is needful," he cried with passionate self-abandonment: " what is my one poor soul to Olive's happiness? "

They wrestled together for an hour. At the end of that time, the Bishop went forth, no more relieved in mind than when he entered. The saintly man had suggested no way out of this hopeless difficulty, save the one hateful way of telling Olive—which made the difficulty. Telling the world as well—that was easy enough to do; but telling Olive also; that was far more impossible.

CHAPTER XXVI.

WHEN he returned to Dorchester, Mrs. Glisson noticed his worn and drawn expression. He had the face of a man who has spent the night in fighting wild beasts at Ephesus. His mouth was rigid; deep wrinkled lines marked the corners of his eyes; his lips were ashy pale; his cheek was colourless.

She asked anxiously what was wrong. He put her off with an evasive answer. No, no, he was quite well; it was only this question of forged orders that was troubling his peace; he *must* get to the bottom of it. He had consulted the Fathers, and would consult them further. Now the question was once raised, he could have no peace as bishop of this diocese till he felt he had settled it. He salved his conscience at the same time by saying to himself that this was literally true; it was indeed a question of forged orders or their equivalent that disturbed his spirit.

His confession, he found, had brought him no nearer the end. For 'twas not of repentance, of forgiveness, of his own poor soul that he thought, but of restitution, of reparation for the wrong he had done, and of Olive. An assurance at that moment that his sin was forgiven would have availed him little. The wrong not the sin it was that troubled him. Forgiveness of his sin would have left Olive untouched. Olive's disillusion was the one dread that haunted him.

He shut himself up in his study once more, and locked the door behind him lest anyone should chance to come in and disturb him. Then he seated himself by his desk, buried his head in his hands, and proceeded to think out this insoluble problem.

The longer he thought of it, the more insoluble it grew. He could only arrive at one conclusion for the moment. Never again from that day forth would he perform any clerical or episcopal function. He was done with lying, and with acting out the lie. How to carry out this resolve he had no clear conception; but the resolve was there. For Olive's sake, he shrank from revealing what he ought to reveal—that he was not and never had been really a clergyman. But at least he could refrain in future from adding to his wrong-doing, and from extending the possible field of evil by ordaining men who were not canonically ordained and by confirming children without proper authority. That meant, of course, that he must resign his see: " His bishopric let another take " rang in his ears perpetually.

And when he reflected (in his honestly professional way) what " a sphere of usefulness " the bishopric afforded him, he was truly sorry for it. But give it up he must. That was the one thing certain. Though it struck him as curious, for all his humility, that he, the one bishop who had never been even a priest, should be the only man on the bench then strenuously engaged in fighting the battle of the poor, the unemployed, the downcast, the miserable. He would have been a good Christian, but for the misfortune of circumstances; what a pity that circumstances must deprive God's poor of their chief protector in the English episcopate!

More than that, he must give up at once every advantage he had gained from his false position. That meant poverty for Olive and Evelyn, of course; but Olive could bear poverty better than disgrace; and as to Evelyn, why Evelyn would shortly marry, and then——

But *would* Evelyn marry? When he came

to think of it, her marriage depended upon young Thornbury receiving that problematical appointment at the Education Office. And his receiving that appointment was dependent again upon the Bishop's recommendation. But the recommendation was effective only because Sir Nathaniel believed that he, Tom Pringle or Cecil Glisson, was and would continue to be Bishop of Dorchester. Supposing to-day he were to write to Sir Nathauiel that he was about to resign his office and let another man take his bishopric, would Sir Nathaniel still think it desirable to appoint young Thornbury? Nay; if this change of front was to be effective at all, must he not try from this moment forth to prevent any new step being taken on any hand which could add to the sum of his unauthorised action? A recommendation to the Education Office was not in itself, to be sure, an episcopal act; but it had been made by him as bishop; and not having taken effect as yet, it must be nipped at once, at whatever hazard.

The Bishop, however, did not act precipitately. Episcopal training militates against precipitancy. He sat long in an absorbed attitude before he proceeded to write that irrevocable letter. But at last he wrote it. Nor did he give away his case and his cause all at once. He wrote, not as one might have expected, in a turmoil of remorse, but carefully, calmly, deliberately, guardedly. He left loop-holes of escape; he abstained from saying the worst with too abrupt an insistence. He explained to Sir Nathaniel that since their last interview a considerable change had come over his convictions. He felt he could no longer be Bishop of Dorchester. "Do not ask," he wrote, "what private reasons have moved me to this tardy resolve. I have not yet made them public, nor do I know whether I shall ever make them public. But the resolve itself exists. It is absolute and imperative. You will conjecture as your first guess that my faith is shaken; in these days of growing doubt, that is a natural inference. But it is nevertheless a wrong one. My convictions as to the fundamental truths of the constitution of the universe remain unaltered. Purely personal and private causes lead me to feel I can no longer fulfil the office of bishop. You will ask, once more, why I ·make *you* in particular the first confidant of this strange determination. I answer, because you are the person of whom, as Bishop, I last asked an official favour. Under all these circumstances, I cannot persist in my recommendation of Mr. Alexander Thornbury of Merton College for an Inspectorship of Church Schools in the diocese of Dorchester. I ask you, therefore, so far as I am concerned, to cancel this recommendation; though I feel it would be wrong in any other way to interfere with Mr. Thornbury's natural chances. He is an able young man, whose merits are wholly outside the present question."

He read the letter over many times before dispatching it. It did not say enough; and yet it said too much. He realised that to send it was to commit himself irrevocably. Yet he would send it for all that; and to make sure of its going, he would even adopt the unusual course of carrying it out himself to the neighbouring post-box—for he was, as you will have perceived, an unconventional bishop. Strange to say, for one of his office, he had no petty pride. He looked about him for a stamp. There were none on the desk. He unlocked the door and called out softly: " Evelyn! "

" Yes, Daddy," Evelyn answered.

Her unconcerned girlish voice smote the Bishop to the quick. Could she have answered so blithely if she knew why he called her? The thought made his voice unusually solemn. " My child," he said in an austere tone, " I want a penny stamp." He said no more than that, but his accent and his look fairly terrified Evelyn.

"Why, Papa, what's the matter?" she cried, looking hard at him. His face was twitching.

"Nothing, nothing, my child," the Bishop answered hastily. "That is to say, nothing physical. I have been troubled, as you know, Evelyn, about this—this question of forged orders; and it has caused me, I confess, much mental agony. I have been writing a letter, my dear, which I wish to post myself; and I want a penny stamp for it."

He spoke with confusion, in a hesitating way which struck Evelyn as doubtful. She snatched up the letter, as it lay, face downward, on the blotting-book. "Why, it's to Sir Nathaniel!" she exclaimed eagerly.

"Ye-es," the Bishop admitted, trembling, "it *is* to Sir Nathaniel."

Evelyn's face flushed fiery red. "This is *my* business," she said, leaning over it and suddenly tearing it open. "Papa, Papa, you haven't said anything foolish?"

"I don't know, Evey," the Bishop answered, thankful this time to circumstances. "I have said—what was inevitable."

Evelyn read the letter all through, and then laid it down, white-faced. In a second, she realised that this was a very serious matter. For Evelyn was no fool. Then, as often happens with girls of her sort, so great a crisis brought out all the latent gentleness of her heart, concealed as a rule under a purely conventional garb of outer flippancy. She was not angry; she was not indignant. She merely bent down a very sobered face and kissed the poor soul-wearied man twice, tenderly, on the forehead.

" If you must send it, Papa," she said slowly, " you must send it."

" I must send it, darling," her father answered, finding suddenly the relief of tears. " But, oh, Evey,—your mother! "

Evelyn looked at him with a bursting heart. " I don't know what it means," she answered. " But it means something very bad. And—it will kill Mother."

" She believes in me so," the poor man burst out, almost yielding up his secret.

" She *ought* to believe in you," Evelyn answered with pride: " for we all believe in you, and we have somebody worth believing in. Daddy, Daddy, I have sometimes made fun of your scruples, but, darling, in my soul I have always honoured them. I have a father and a mother I can respect from my heart; and I *know* you can have done nothing Mother and I could be ashamed of."

She flung her arms round his neck and kissed

him, passionately. But just at that second, such a declaration of faith, made from a full heart in a moment of emotion, was the very worst blow the poor wavering Bishop could have received. If only she had reproached him! He wiped his brow and held her off from him, trembling, as though afraid lest he should pollute her. "My child, my child," he cried, in his agony of self-abasement, "you lacerate me, with your kindness. You are wrong; you are wrong. I have done things to plunge your mother and yourself into shame and misery. You could be angry with me and sin not."

"I don't believe it," Evelyn answered stoutly.

The Bishop groaned. "But it is true," he reiterated. "Yet, Evey, for heaven's sake, don't let your mother know it. I didn't mean to tell *you;* but if *she* were to know, it would kill her; it would kill her."

"She doesn't know; she shall never know," Evelyn cried. "And whatever it is, it isn't true; I know that beforehand. You didn't do it; I know you couldn't; or if you did it, it was right and good, though all the world and all the churches as well were to rise and say it was anathema maranatha. I know you well enough to know this, dear Daddy—that whatever you do is right, right, right; and that even if I thought it wrong till I knew you had done it, I should see it was right when I could know and understand exactly *how* you came to do it."

The Bishop rose, agitated. Her faith in him almost seemed to justify him to himself. He took her in his arms and kissed her passionately. "My child," he said, quivering, "if you knew all, I think you *would* forgive me. You would see how it was forced upon me by a strange concurrence of circumstance. But your mother— your dear mother—who has trusted me so long and believed in me so fully, how can I ever tell her?"

"She is an angel!" Evelyn cried. "And I have behaved like a little beast to her all my life. I see that now. Mother, dear Mother—she must never know. Tell *me*, if you like; but never tell Mother. I can bear anything; I am strong enough and young enough, and I know I shall understand. But Mother, who trusts you—her trust is not like mine; *she* trusts you because she thinks you are incapable of doing the things she believes to be wrong; *I* trust you because I know that even if you did the things I once thought wrong, it is *you* who have done them. And that makes them all right. It guarantees them, so to speak. You know I care nothing for your rules and your laws. It is the man I care for. Not what a man does, but what he is, stamps him. If a man whom I know to be as good as you does anything that seems wrong, I know there must be a difference in the way he does it. That's all very modern and wicked, I dare say, but it's the way I'm built. So you can tell me all. Whatever it is, I know beforehand I shall sympathise."

The Bishop sank into his chair, covered his face with his hands once more, and burst out with a low wail: " Evey, Evey, I am not a clergyman. I was never ordained at all. I am a mere pretender."

Evelyn bent over him wildly, caught him hard in her arms, and kissed him with a sudden flood of desperate tears. " Is that all? ". she cried, half laughing. " Only that, dear Daddy? "

"*All?* " the Bishop exclaimed, aghast, drawing back, and staring at her. " What do you mean by *all?* Isn't that bad enough, Evey? "

Evelyn hugged him in her relief. " Oh, if that's all," she answered, drawing her breath, " I don't mind about *that*. I thought it was much worse:—something really dreadful, don't you know—something that would have worried and killed dear Mother—something about someone else—you understand what I mean, Daddy! "

The Bishop stared at her in surprise. He

did not realise that her mind had turned at once,
as a woman's mind always turns at the vague
suggestion of impending evil, to woman's worst
bugbear—superseded affection. Evelyn had
jumped at the conclusion that there was a woman
in it somewhere. A mere ecclesiastical doubt
was to her quite trifling.

"This is worse, darling, worse," the Bishop
cried, shaking his head solemnly. "Evelyn, I
am not in orders at all. I may have sinned the
unforgivable sin, who knows?—Not that I mind
for that, but for your mother, darling."

Evelyn hugged him again wildly. "Oh,
that's nothing," she answered; "let the unforgivable sin go:" for she had truly said that she
was not bishopy. "If it's only that, I don't care
a pin. I was afraid it was much worse—a previous marriage, perhaps;—or another woman;
one reads about such things in books: though
even then, I should have known it was *you*, and
understood everything: and we might have managed to keep her away for always from dear
Mother. But if it's only false orders, it was accident, of course. I don't need you to explain;
I *know* about it all in my heart already."

The Bishop began to tell her in a very few
words the tale of the John Wesley. Evelyn listened to his story with evident impatience.

"Don't bother about details, dear," she cried. "We must only think now about sparing Mother. You have written that letter, and you had better post it. It will ease your mind, I dare say. Never mind about Alex. We can wait. I'll get you a penny stamp, and then I'll run out with it."

The Bishop clutched it hard. "No, no," he said; "you won't, my child. I shall post it myself. I won't trust it to anybody. I have begun this matter, and now I shall pull through with it."

Evelyn noted the way he clutched it, and her suspicion deepened. "Very well, dear," she answered. "I'll get you the stamp; and then, you and I will go out and post it together."

The Bishop felt relieved even by this partial confession. He leaned back in his chair and looked up at the ceiling. When Evelyn returned with the stamp, she found him still gazing, with his eyes on vacancy, and muttering to himself incoherently: "the sin of Korah, Dathan, and Abiram. They and all that appertained to them went down alive into the pit, and the earth closed upon them; and they perished from among the congregation."

CHAPTER XXVII.

EVELYN ACTS.

As they returned from the post, Evelyn caught sight suddenly of a well-known figure, in a grey tweed suit, hurrying up from the railway station.

She started in surprise and rushed up to the wearer of the suit, excited. "Why, Alex!" she exclaimed, forgetting to be flippant. "And without telegraphing beforehand to tell me you were coming!"

"I didn't know I could manage it, darling, till I passed through Birmingham. It was a close fit of two trains, and I was afraid of disappointing you. But I'm on my way to town, to see Sir Nathaniel Merriton. He has written to make me an appointment for an interview. So I expect it's all right—unless, of course, when he sees me, he doesn't like the look of me."

"He couldn't help liking the look of you—unless he was a donkey; which he isn't, I know, but a dear; a second class dear, you stupid; the middle-aged sort of dear that you needn't look like that over."

"But, Evey, what's the matter? You've been crying, I can see, and you look so worried."

Evelyn drew him down towards the river, behind the bushes of the shrubbery, where she sank on a garden seat, and burst into tears immediately. The very unwontedness of such conduct on her part, as the modern young lady, made it only the more impressive.

"Darling," she exclaimed, all her bravado failing her, "a dreadful thing is happening; and nobody else knows. I'm so glad you've come, to help me and advise me. This bother about the parson at Reading who wasn't in orders at all is unhinging Daddy's mind. I don't know what has happened to him. He thinks he isn't a clergyman himself at all. I'm afraid to leave him one minute alone, for fear he should tell Mother. So far, he has told no one but myself, I believe; but this morning he's full of it. He ran over to Oxford before breakfast, like a madman, and came back quite flurried. He's firmly convinced he has done the same thing himself, and committed the sin of Korah, Dathan, and A-what's-his-name."

Alex took her hand in his. "Dearest," he

whispered very low; " and I thought I was coming to make you so happy."

" So you do, Alex; so you do; I love to have you with me: but, it's so dreadful about Daddy. And do you know what he's just done—posted a letter to Sir Nathaniel to say that he withdraws his recommendation."

Alex whistled to himself. " That's bad," he answered. " We must counteract that. Though I suppose of course he gave the real reason."

" Yes, in part; but not quite as badly as he gave it to me. Not so definitely I mean. He dealt more in generalities. But I can see his mind is going; I've been afraid of it for weeks. I never knew him worry, not even over the chain-makers' strike at Cradley, as he's worried over this business. And he came to me this morning with the wildest story. Oh, quite an absurd story! "

" About himself? "

" Yes. He says he isn't himself at all, but some other person. A common sailor. You know, there was a man blown up by those pirate people in the Pacific somewhere when Daddy was nearly killed;—I've heard the story so often that I forget the details—and it told upon him terribly at the time, I've heard Mums say, so that he could never be induced to allude to it afterwards. Well, that was one thing that unhinged his mind a little once; and now, this other thing coming up, he's gone back to that again, and declares he isn't himself at all, that his name was never Cecil Glisson, and that he's really this dead sailor, Tom Pringle or something."

" What an extraordinary idea! But, Evey, you ought at once to see a doctor."

" It would break Mother's heart. And then, the disgrace of it! "

" But you can't keep it all to yourself. Other people must know soon. And the trouble is too much for you. You *must* have advice about it."

" When do you go up to town? "

" To-morrow morning, darling. I suppose I can sleep here? "

" Of course. Oh, I *am* so glad you came. Yes, I'll do as you say. I'll go up with you to-morrow."

" But your mother——"

" Mother or no; this is no time to stand upon trifles. Besides, chaperons are abolished: Madge says they're an anachronism. I'll go with you, Alex; and I'll see Sir Nathaniel."

" Evey, you're sure it's a delusion? You're sure he has fancies? It can't be true? You see, we mustn't force his hand,—drive him into a confession, must we? "

"Alex, do you think I don't know my own father better than that—the dear darling? Why, he *couldn't* tell a lie, not if his life depended on it. Even now, in this delusion, he never thinks of himself; he thinks only of the effect upon me and Mother. It's just a freak of conscience. He has brooded on the wickedness of this man at Reading so long that he begins to believe he's done the same himself. But he couldn't do it, poor dear; he's a vast deal too innocent. Why, he couldn't go on with it for two days together. He'd let it out in half an hour; he could never keep up a great organised deception. Though if he'd really done it, it wouldn't much matter either; for whatever he does, it's his nature to do it for sufficient reasons."

"Evey, what faith you have! You are a true woman."

"Faith in the men I love, Alex; yes, faith to the very end. Not faith that they'll never do wrong; I don't care for that kind; but faith in them still even if I know they have done it. I told him so just now. It doesn't matter to me whether it's true or not, so far as that goes. He's still himself. And do you think something he once did before I was born is going to blot out the memory of all these years that I have lived and *known* him—the memory of what he is and always has been? I should think of him the same if you could prove to me this minute that he committed a murder in New South Wales thirty years ago. I should say: ' Poor dear; what could have driven him to do it?'"

CHAPTER XXVIII.

OFFICIAL INTELLIGENCE.

By the first train next morning, Evelyn went up to Paddington. In these latter days of the decline and fall of the chaperon, on which she had insisted, her mother did not even attempt to prevent her. The bicycle has entailed a general decadence of chaperonage. She went openly with Alex, and accompanied him to the door of the Education Office. There, she sent up her card to Sir Nathaniel, with the pencilled words "A. T. is here also; but *he* can wait. My need is urgent."

In a few minutes, a Private Secretary with a most official face, a big black moustache, and a languid drawl, came down to the waiting room. "Sir Nathaniel will see you at once," he drawled out. Very pale and trembling, Evelyn followed him up to the great man's sanctum.

As soon as the door was closed, Sir Nathaniel leaned back in his revolving chair, folded his hands before him, and stared hard in her face with comical resignation. "So you are bent upon making a job of it?" he murmured slowly. "You mean to turn out the Government! Are you aware, my dear young lady, that this action of yours makes the appointment of your protégé —let us call him your protégé still—it prevents complications—absolutely impossible?"

Evelyn half broke down; tears floated in her eyes. "Oh, Sir Nathaniel," she burst out, "I haven't come about that. I've come about Papa. A terrible thing has happened. Have you read his letter?"

"God bless my soul, no," the Secretary answered, astonished. "Is it as bad as all that?" He turned over a great pile of correspondence that lay littered in front of him. "Here it is," he said, "unread. Tutnell told me it was important; but I haven't had time to glance at it." He skimmed through it hastily. Then his face grew graver. "Well, what does this mean?" he asked, with a dim misgiving. It seemed to forbode evil. He half suspected what Evelyn herself had fancied—an open scandal. Could the Bishop have run away with some other man's housemaid?"

"Papa wrote that letter," Evelyn said, schooling herself to talk calmly, "under the influence of—well, very intense emotion. I saw it when he had finished; and I'm afraid—Sir Nathaniel, help me out with this, do; I'm afraid he wrote it in a fit of delusion."

"Clearly," Sir Nathaniel answered with the promptitude of an official whose business it is to explain away everything.

"Well,—that's all," Evelyn said, and glanced up at him tearfully.

She looked so much prettier, so much tenderer, so much more womanly that day, in her simple morning dress with her tearful eyes, than he had ever before seen her that Sir Nathaniel was touched. He rose and moved over toward her. Then he laid one hand on her shoulder and took hers in the other. He was a kind old friend, and Evelyn let him hold it.

"My poor child," he said, in a voice of unwonted softness, "that is enough. I see it clearly now. This trouble about that rascal at Reading has told upon his overworked brain. But we may set all straight yet. Does Mrs. Glisson know of it?"

"No," Evelyn answered. "Thank Heaven, no." She had grown into a woman at once. "And I want to spare her," she went on. "If she knows, it will kill her. Daddy has been everything in the world to Mother. Nobody has heard but myself. I only tell *you* because he wrote that letter. I want you to take no notice; and I want you to advise me what to do about it."

Sir Nathaniel took counsel with his watch. He was accustomed to acting with promptitude. "Is young Thornbury here now?" he asked.

"Yes. He came up to town with me."

Sir Nathaniel hummed and hawed, and beat a devil's tattoo with his fingers on the table. "He mustn't stop," he answered, after a deliberative pause. "Under the circumstances, it would be impossible for me to see him to-day. Let me think; he must go; but where can he meet you later? Say at the confectioner's at the bottom of Regent Street. You know it, I suppose. That will do, won't it?"

"Perfectly," Evelyn answered.

The great man wrote three lines and placed them in an envelope. Then he rang a hand-bell. "For Mr. Thornbury," he said; "in the waiting room below; to cancel appointment."

The Private Secretary took it and nodded.

"Now, look here, Evey," Sir Nathaniel went on—"I may call you Evey, mayn't I, as I'm just going to disappoint you? You are a young lady who thoroughly understands official language."

"I trust so," Evelyn answered with a faint access of hope.

"Yes, you do," the man of office said, clinching it. "And you also understand official necessities. Most girls are born fools; you happen to belong to the opposite category. You will see at once that your coming here this morning with Mr. Thornbury and trying to see me was extremely ill-timed. In point of fact, fatal. Therefore I should like to assure you categorically that before you arrived—last night in fact—I had already made up my mind *not* to appoint Mr. Thornbury, but another person. To that resolution I must adhere. Do you thoroughly comprehend me?"

He looked her full in the face. His eyes met hers. Evelyn glanced at them from under her eyelids with unwonted timidity. Even *her* irreverent soul was awed for the moment by the gravity of the situation. "I—I think I follow," she faltered dubiously.

"I'm not quite sure that you do," Sir Nathaniel answered, laying his hand again gently on the poor child's shoulder. "I'm sorry to disappoint you, Evey; but—exigencies of state, you know: the service is the service, and the country is exacting. Therefore, your friend must not expect this appointment."

Evelyn lifted her eyes timidly. "Oh, thank you," she said with a very short gasp.

Sir Nathaniel froze. "There is nothing at all to thank me for; quite the contrary," he answered.

Evelyn smiled in spite of herself. "Then thank you for nothing," she broke out with a spice of her usual devilry.

"That's better; that's better! *Now* we understand one another. You will break it to young Thornbury—unofficially, of course? That's excellect—excellent. Evey, you're one of the most intelligent and sensible girls I know. If you were a man, I think I would appoint you my private secretary. You have a head on your shoulders."

"Thank you again, Sir Nathaniel."

The official smiled coldly. But the corner of his eye belied his mouth. It was almost human. "Well, having dismissed that point for ever," he said dryly, " and made it quite clear that nothing can be done, we may as well get on to the other business. Stop; one moment; before we pass on, tell Thornbury that he had better say nothing about it. I think I shall now delay the appointment for a fortnight, in order to make enquiries about suitable persons. You may tell him—not from me, but as a private hint from yourself,—that you believe the other man will receive the post, let us say in ten days or so."

Evelyn nodded her head. "Oh, thank you, thank you."

"Not at all," Sir Nathaniel continued. "I wish you wouldn't say thank you. It's embarrassing, very. Such a compromising word. If Tutnell happened to come in, he might foolishly suppose I had been promising you something. And it is against our principles in this office ever to make any promises to anybody."

"I will take care not to countenance such a foolish misconception," Evelyn replied demurely.

"That's well," the official went on. "Now, let us talk about your father. This is bad news, Evey. I'm distressed to hear it."

Evelyn broke down again, this time sobbing outright. Sir Nathaniel leant over her in comical agitation. "My dear child," he cried, "my dear child, not *that*, whatever you do! Suppose somebody were to come in? So very unofficial!"

Evelyn did her best to dry her eyes, not quite successfully. Sir Nathaniel bent over her, and tried to soothe her. After a while she grew calmer, and told her little story as well as she was able, suppressing part, but mentioning enough to let the Secretary judge the gravity of the situation. He listened attentively; then he said at last: "Of course this is all delusion. His letter to me shows even that he had not fully made up his mind at the moment when he wrote, what particular form the delusion should take. It is vague and general. But I don't think there is cause for any serious alarm. Your father is not a man of the insane temperament. He has systematically overworked himself, and may have a passing attack like this, due to nothing more than disordered nerves. But he will never go mad; you may take my word for it."

"You think not?" Evelyn cried, grasping at this ray of hope with profuse gratitude.

"No, certainly not," the man of experience answered. "Remember, I was a doctor myself before I went into politics; and I can tell you one thing about madness that may comfort you. Insanity is a disease of the selfish temperament. It occurs only or almost only among the self-centred. Go to an asylum any day and hear what the patients have to tell you; it is I, I, I, from beginning to end. Never some other person. *I* am the Queen of England, *I* am the prophet Mahomet, *I* am the Archbishop of Canterbury, *I* have come into a large sum of money, *I* am in the depths of misery and destitution, *I* am being persecuted by the police, *I* am the victim of a conspiracy which haunts me everywhere. But not one patient is ever thinking, That man there is the Emperor of Germany; that woman is the wife of the prophet Mahomet; my friends are being persecuted; my son or my cousin has come into an immense fortune. It is all as personal as personal can be; no love, no sympathy, no thought for others."

"That's not in the least like Daddy," Evelyn answered with conviction. "Whatever is the matter, he is always the same—the most unselfish of men. He thinks about Mums, about me, about the chain-makers, about his poor people, till I sometimes feel inclined to say: 'Oh, bother the poor, Daddy; do remember that you too have a soul to save and a body to take care of!' Even since this began I can see it's the marriages he has performed and the people he has ordained that most of all trouble him. He never thinks of himself; he thinks about the scandal and the disgrace to the episcopacy, and the way dear Mother would be horrified to learn it."

"Then you may be sure it will pass," Sir Nathaniel said with promptitude. "That is not serious madness. Madness has only two springs: one is selfishness, pure piggish selfishness: the other is like unto it—stolid family placidity. A man of varied interests *never* goes mad. And I'll tell you what you'd better do; you'd better get Yate-Westbury to run down with you accidentally, and report upon your father. Stop a minute!" Sir Nathaniel consulted his watch once more. "Shall I? Yes, hang it all, I *will;* I can talk out the deputation in twenty minutes. Sheer politeness will do it: agree with them all round, and commit myself to nothing. The deputation withdraws, much pleased with its reception. There's a train at a quarter to three. I could catch that, I think. I know Yate-Westbury. I'll go round and drag him away, patients or no patients. Your father's condition is clearly critical; and such a man as he is worth many sparrows. Yate-Westbury's patients are mostly jackdaws. Yate-Westbury must come. I'll meet you at Paddington. Now, off to your disappointed friend, and break the news to him gently that he must give up all hopes of obtaining an inspectorship!" He bowed her out with a soft touch on the shoulder.

Ten minutes later Evelyn was lunching with Alex at a café in Regent Street, and exclaiming with effusion: "Well, Alex, Sir Nathaniel's the greatest dear, bar one, that ever was born! He's been just sweet to me. And he told me, officially you know,—I mean, in official topsy-turvey—that in spite of Daddy's letter you should have the inspectorship before the end of a fortnight."

CHAPTER XXIX.

THE BISHOP TURNS.

THEY travelled down to Dorchester together —Sir Nathaniel, Yate-Westbury, Evelyn, and Alex Thornbury, the only four people, save old Dr. Littlemore, who had learned the secret of the Bishop's delusion.

The great specialist was very consoling, on the way, to Evelyn. He made light of the danger. It was arranged that he should assume the part of a person who had come down in search of a building site somewhere near the river, and should be introduced to the Palace by Sir Nathaniel, who was supposed to have met him casually at the station. This would prevent unnecessary alarm on the patient's part. But Yate-Westbury echoed Sir Nathaniel's own opinion as to the Bishop's state of mind. He made Evelyn retail to him her father's symptoms; then he leaned back at last on the padded cushions of his first class carriage and answered with easy conviction: " Oh, there can't be much the matter with *him*, Miss Glisson. It doesn't take them so. Not that way madness lies. A passing hysterical illusion, perhaps; no more. He'll get better of it soon with rest and change—a month in the Engadine. Dismiss the trouble from your mind for the present. I'll tell you more about it after I've had a chat with him."

At the station, they separated. Evelyn and Alex walked up by themselves to the Palace; Sir Nathaniel and Yate-Westbury drove after them in a fly twenty minutes later. Might they see the Bishop? The Bishop, much perturbed, came out into the drawing-room to see them.

Sir Nathaniel played his part like a diplomatist that he was. He had run down to call upon the Bishop about that little matter of the letter, which had somewhat disquieted him; but at the same time, he had happened to meet at the station his friend Mr. Augustus Egerton, a North Country manufacturer—"you know the firm—Wells, Egerton, and Backhouse," he interposed in a stage aside—who was looking out for a place on the river where he could build a bungalow and a suitable boat-house for his electric launch. He wanted some pretty reach within easy distance of Oxford. "I've ventured to bring him along with me," he said, "knowing that you were a good authority as to this part of the country; and besides "—confidentially, in another stage whisper, "the diocese of Dorchester, you know:—no large industrial towns—rich men are not abundant; so if you fixed him here betimes, you might see the completion of the new transept."

. The Bishop turned to him with a troubled far-away smile. "Thank you," he said slowly, "thank you. I have much to think about. But stone and mortar are the least. And the transept is *not* just now my first object."

They strolled out upon the lawn through the open window. Yate-Westbury began asking some perfunctory questions as to land and houses and depth of water in-shore for steam launches to approach, which the Bishop answered in the same pre-occupied manner. It was clear his mind was not in the subject. But gradually they drew apart round the far end of the shrubbery. There, close to the spot where Birinus had baptised the first Christians in Wessex, the Bishop dropped into a seat, and to Yate-Westbury's immense surprise, turned with sudden fierceness on his unexpected visitor. "This is a plot," he said bitterly. "A mean, lying plot. An attempt against my sanity. I know you, sir: I know you. Evelyn should not have done this. It is a wicked conspiracy."

The specialist eyed him hard. His mind was shaken at first from the decision he had given beforehand to Miss Glisson. Conspiracy—a plot? Surely the very vocabulary of madness!

"Why, how do you mean?" he asked in his most honeyed and candid manner—with the mock candour of the mad doctor, transparently artificial.

The Bishop astonished him by flaring out his answer at once. "Yes, a conspiracy, I tell you; and I am not well pleased that my daughter should have contrived it. She is driving me to bay, and heaven only knows what misfortune may come of it—for my poor dear wife, to spare whom I would gladly die in torture. Ah, you think I don't know you; but I do, very well. I saw through this thing the moment Sir Nathaniel introduced you just now under an assumed name. You are not Mr. Egerton; you are Dr. Yate-Westbury, the specialist on insanity. I sat with you nine months ago on the same platform at a meeting in St. James's Hall; and I have seen you since more than once in the street in London."

The specialist was taken aback. "Oh, indeed?" was all he could answer. "I go about a good deal up and down in England."

"Yes; and you have come here to-day to see

whether I am mad. Well, Dr. Yate-Westbury, I wish to heaven I was. It would save a great deal of misery to everybody. But I am worse than mad; that would be disgrace enough in itself for my poor wife and daughter; yet not so bad as the disgrace I must ultimately bring upon them. What has Evelyn told you? Let me hear that first. She is driving me hard, and I must know how far she has driven me in this matter."

" Miss Glisson merely said," the specialist answered, making a clear breast of it, " that you had told her what she frankly described as a cock-and-bull story, about your life in Melanesia; that the cock-and-bull story was so obviously false that it had alarmed her for your safety; and that acting on Sir Nathaniel Merriton's advice,—very sound advice, as a rule—she wished me to see you and to report upon your sanity. There now, you observe, I have unreservedly exposed the whole wicked conspiracy. I have been perfectly frank with you; be frank with me in return, and tell me the nature of this trouble that weighs upon you."

The Bishop turned upon him and looked him through and through. " Dr. Yate-Westbury," he said slowly, " this is no case for you, but for a higher tribunal. It was asked long ago of one of your sort, ' Canst thou minister to a mind diseased?' and the disease was of the same kind as with me,—remorse, and horror for wrong done, irrevocable. What that wrong was, I am not going to tell you. My daughter has not told you; for that crumb of comfort I am grateful to Providence. I have lain awake all night long, wondering whether the easiest way out of it would not be by flinging myself here into the river. I am a good swimmer; I could stem the weir there: yet I am sure I have self-control enough to abstain from swimming, even when I felt the death-gurgle fighting in my throat, if that were necessary for my wife's and my daughter's happiness. But I have weighed suicide in the balance, and come to the conclusion that suicide is not the best way out. What I say to you now, I say in confidence. I have wrestled in prayer all night long, beseeching the Lord to let me die before this secret is out, for my wife's sake and my daughter's; and I almost feel as though my prayer would be answered. I have not prayed for forgiveness for myself, but that my sin should not be visited on those innocent heads. But I cannot kill myself, for their sake, though to kill myself would perhaps be the safest way in the end to save them. That is all I think about. If only I could die, and still keep this secret, everything would be well. But Evelyn is making it hard for the secret to be kept. The very wife and child for whose sake I would die, carrying my secret with me, are striving their best to drag the truth out of me."

Yate-Westbury leaned forward with professional interest and watched the patient closely. He was probing the man's eyes, scanning the twitch of his mouth, noting his eager fingers. By dexterous side-questions—seeming to agree, seeming to differ—acquiescing, expostulating—the great specialist slowly drew him out. On the subject of his supposed sin, the Bishop firmly declined to say anything; he was reticence itself; he merely declared that he had made up his mind irrevocably never again to perform any sacred office. "I put the thing from me," he said succinctly. But on the subject of his general health, his devotion to Olive and Evelyn, his remorse and anguish, he was articulate and even voluble. He did not wish to be thought mad; and he knew himself sane. The stigma on Evelyn alone would have deterred him from seeking that outlet. Nay more, it was part of his penance that he must endure his punishment; and if the punishment came, he would endure it manfully. But to be taken for mad would be to shirk the penalty: nor could he have Evelyn falsely branded as a madman's daughter. What he had done he would pay for; but he would not let his innocent daughter pay for what he had never done, nor been, nor dreamt of.

He spoke long and earnestly. Yate-Westbury listened with keen professional eagerness. At the end of the interview, the doctor went off to seek the man of office. Sir Nathaniel was in the drawing-room, stretching his big legs uneasily in a long wicker chair, and trying to make conversation with Mrs. Glisson and Evelyn. Yate-Westbury drew him aside and beckoned him out on to the lawn. They paused behind the lilacs. "Well?" Sir Nathaniel said enquiringly. "You find his brain touched?"

Yate-Westbury's confident answer came with crushing force. "No; not in the least degree; the man's as sane as you are. Whatever it was, he has really done it."

"You are sure?"

"Never was more certain of a case in my life. The symptoms are obvious. Remorse, not madness. I've watched his face, his eyes, his gestures. He's deeply agitated, acting under the influence of some profound emotion; but it's strictly normal. Emotion, I should say, of an overpowering character, affecting a man built on the exact opposite lines from the insane temperament—a many-sided, wholesome, hard-working, honest, well-meaning man, who has been hurried into some crime, perhaps a small one, and is suffering for it exaggerated regret and agony."

Sir Nathaniel gave a long low "Whew!" "That's bad," he answered, stopping dead short: "about as bad as it can be. The other thing would be better. If he isn't mad, my dear fellow, he's—well, whatever he is, he's not a bishop."

"You think it——"

"Yes: criminal."

There was a long pause. Then they talked it over for a while, Sir Nathaniel, on second thoughts, regretting at once his hasty admission. "At least," he said after a while, "you will treat this expression of opinion as confidential. You are here professionally, and you will not divulge a professional secret. We may save a scandal yet. What will you say to Miss Glisson?"

"The simple truth; it is always easiest. 'I have examined your father, and find him perfectly sane and normal. He is suffering merely from excessive emotion.' She must put her own explanation upon it."

CHAPTER XXX.

THE BISHOP DECIDES.

It was Saturday evening. Sir Nathaniel and Yate-Westbury spent the night at the Palace. The great specialist had doubts at first whether it was well for him to stay; he feared lest his presence might be misinterpreted both by the Bishop and by others. But Evelyn settled the question for him with the imperiousness of her age and generation. " You must stop," she said quietly. " It's better for Daddy, and better for Mums too. You have reassured our minds; and whatever is the matter with him, he's not afraid of *you*. So you had better wait on and see how he is in the morning."

It was a gloomy dinner party. The cloud brooded over them all. Evelyn and Alex made a vain pretence of keeping things lively; and the man of politics tried to engage the Bishop in talk about the progress of events in that eternal East, which resembles the poor in being always with us. But nothing could dispel the deep gloom that had settled on the Bishop. He ate his dinner in silence, conscious of doom, and with the fate of thousands of souls weighing down his conscience. Worst of all, he had still the deadly problem of Olive. As she sat and faced him, with her calm middle-aged comeliness, as beautiful in his eyes that evening as when he saw her first on the verandah at Sydney, he could not conceive how he was ever to break the truth to her. That he had never been; that she had never married him; that all their life together was a lie and a delusion! No wonder he shrank from that terrible confession, that the man she had loved, had honoured, had married, was utterly non-existent, and that in his place stood a mendacious run-away sailor, masquerading as priest, as bishop, and as philanthropist.

That he *was* all these save in the accident of ordination was nothing to the purpose. He was too ecclesiasticised himself, and had too much trained his wife to the ecclesiastical standpoint, for that to matter to either of them.

The Bishop retired early. He went to his own room, not because he hoped for sleep,—sleep was now a rare visitor—but because he thought it easier at least to be alone than to make the hateful pretence of talking about trifles when his soul was elsewhere. He locked his door and knelt down to pray. Not originally or by instinct a religious man, prayer had become to him with time a professional reality. He had grown devout by mere clerical habit. It was his nature to throw himself vividly into all that he undertook. He had never allowed the irregularity of his manner of entering the fold to interfere with his whole-hearted acceptance of the priestly position once he was within it. He had always prayed; of late, indeed, he had prayed without ceasing. He acknowledged to heaven, as he acknowledged to himself, the wrongfulness of his deception; he was too honest in soul to palter with omnipotence: but he trusted that the Searcher of hearts, in whom he fully believed, knowing all, would make allowance for the subtlety and strength of the temptation. It was without fear, therefore, that the Bishop threw himself on his knees before the Throne of Grace; he was praying from his heart, an earnest prayer for others; and that prayer he felt sure the worst of men might pray without sin at so fateful a crisis.

He did not pray for himself,—for forgiveness, for heaven, for some way out of his difficulties. He was utterly oblivious of his own salvation. He prayed for Olive; he prayed for Evelyn. He wrestled with his Lord that his innocent wife and child might be spared this humiliation. For himself, he had sinned, and he was willing to expiate that sin with whatever punishment Eternal Justice might see fit to inflict upon him; but he prayed, with trembling lips, that the sins of the fathers might not be visited on the children, that the innocent wife might not suffer for the guilty husband. He prayed with a solemn dread, for he remembered only too well that his was the sin of Korah, Dathan, and Abiram, and that Korah, Dathan, and Abiram had been swallowed alive by the earth, not themselves alone, but with all that appertained to them. Yet he wrestled none the less, with great drops of perspiration standing on his brow. He begged hard to be punished to the utmost of his sin, both here and hereafter, if only these little ones might not suffer with him.

It was a terrible expiation. He endured it like a man. His one thought throughout was that he must save his beloved ones.

Hour after hour he prayed on, with feverish eagerness. Then slowly, out of the darkness, a gleam of light came to him. He saw it visibly stealing over the tower of the Cathedral. Day was dawning, and hope dawned with it.

He knew not why he had this sudden sense of unaccountable relief—this strange feeling that somehow all would yet be well with him. Well, that is to say, rather, with Olive and Evelyn. But he *did* feel it for all that; a curious instinct which seemed to tell him he was doomed himself —that his body should pay in endless torture for his sin—but that Olive and Evelyn should be spared that last misery of a broken idol. For a while he was calmer; something in his head made him feel light and at peace. He did not sleep, indeed, or desire to sleep; but he lay back in his easy chair, closed his eyes, and thought more calmly. Had his prayer been answered? Were Olive and Evelyn to be saved from this exposure?

All night he had sat and watched by the open window: as the light grew clearer above the Cathedral tower, his heart grew happier each moment. He knew not why, but he had confidence that his prayer had been heard. Yet he was dimly conscious too that he must make reparation. And how could he make reparation save only by confession? And how could he confess save by ruining Olive's life for her? If he could but die! He leaned out of the window, and saw the river flow fast past the spot where Birinus had brought the faith of Christ to Wessex. In that river he could expiate his sin no doubt—and save Olive. But what a poor way of saving her! To leave to her and Evelyn the stigma of a suicide's widow and orphan—no, no, he shrank from it. Easy enough to drown, of course; but what would come after drowning? Not for himself, not for himself; he would welcome hell, if hell were the appointed way for him to make Olive happy, and to expiate his crime; he was manly enough to wish to bear his proper penalty. But for Olive? No, no; that was not the way the Power that rules the affairs of men had ordained for her delivery. He would have faith that it would come; and come it would with morning.

And with morning it came. A messenger at the door, post haste from Oxford.

About five o'clock the Bishop had felt that strange sense of relief. And about five o'clock there had died suddenly at Oxford the one man to whom he had told the whole tale of his deception, Dr. Littlemore of Oriel.

He knew instinctively, as he opened the letter which the messenger brought, that it was a message from the grave. He read it through in silence. " Dr. Littlemore died this morning at five. In his last moments, seized suddenly with a spasm of heart disease, he was inarticulately anxious about the safety of your soul, and about some evil which he expected the Church to suffer from you. He could not be happy till I had promised him that the moment he was dead I would send a messenger at once to tell you so. He murmured frequently, ‘Tell the Bishop of Dorchester he must confess before men. As he sinned before men, so must he confess, openly.’ I have no idea to what our dear friend referred, and I have little doubt he was labouring under a delusion. But as he made me promise him most solemnly that I would report his words at once, I am sure you will forgive my bringing a dying man's last wish to your immediate notice." It was signed by a scarcely less famous Canon of Christ Church.

Then the Bishop knew all. He saw his Lord's way, and with a deadly struggle, he endeavoured to accept it.

He cast himself down on his knees once more, and prayed with all his soul that this trial might pass from him. But the longer he prayed, the more profoundly did the sense steal over him that he must tell all out—must confess to Olive. If she was to hear it at all, she would hear it better from his own lips than from any other's. Yet how was he to tell her? Well, well, we must quit us like men, whatever happens; and the Bishop felt now that to quit himself like a man was all that was left for him. He rose from his knees once more with a profound sense of a duty imposed upon him. He would drink his cup to the dregs, and save Olive what he could of this unspeakable exposure.

With a whirling head, he staggered rather than walked into the breakfast room, and shook hands mechanically with Yate-Westbury and Sir Nathaniel. Although he shook hands with them, he was not conscious of their presence. Then he turned to his wife, who had spent the night in her own room, almost as sleepless as himself. To stand near Olive was like coming to anchor after a storm. "Olive, dearest," he said, with his never-failing tenderness more apparent than ever, "I want to speak alone with you. I must speak at once—in the study—before breakfast. No, Evelyn, no—" for Evelyn darted forward with a glance of deprecating horror; "I must have this out now alone with your mother; there is no other way possible." He waved her aside gently, and took his wife's hand in his own. "Come, darling," he said, in a soothing voice. "Come with me to the study. I have something to say. And—I had better say it."

Mrs. Glisson followed him into the study with a strange foreboding. The Bishop seated her in a chair, and knelt beside her, with his face laid against her, like a lover. For a moment he was silent. The same pressure in his head which he noticed during the night oppressed and numbed him. But he began very softly. "Olive," he said, "my Olive, for nearly thirty years we have lived together. We have loved each other dearly. You have been to me the best wife God ever gave any man. You have sympathised with my work; you have been light and warmth to me. I love you now as I have loved you ever, more than I think any other man can ever have loved and honoured the woman that God gave him. To cause you a moment's pain has always been hateful to me. I cannot bear to think "—he paused and hesitated, stroking her hand meanwhile with infinite tenderness. "Olive," he said once more, "I love you so profoundly that—that —that," he let her hand drop suddenly and leant his head against her once more. "My darling," he whispered, "my dar—my d-d-d——" The words stuck in his throat. He could get no further.

With a terrible effort, he strove to speak; but speech would not come to him. He tried to move his tongue. It was tied and immovable. A sudden burst of meaning told him all was up. He knew now what it meant. This was clearly paralysis.

And he could see the meaning of that sense

of relief in his head about five o'clock that morning. A small blood-vessel on the brain must have given way then, and a second one this moment. His speech was gone. He *could not* confess to Olive!

But he *must!* But he *must!* Or at least he must try. Though God grant his trying fail! Yet at least he must make the effort.

He prayed hard for failure. He, who had never once prayed for success, accepting it passively. But he staggered towards the table, and seized a pen with manful resolution.

Trembling and dazed, he wrote down the first few words of an attempted confession, which came to nothing. But before the first line was finished, his hand had dropped by his side. He could do no more. Arm and tongue both failed him.

He stood there, mumbling. Mrs. Glisson rang the bell and called loudly for help. Sir Nathaniel and Yate-Westbury came at once at her cry; so, a minute later, did Alex and Evelyn.

They carried the Bishop to bed. He lay on his pillow, very quiet. Though unable to speak or move, he was conscious of all that was passing around him. Yate-Westbury bent over him and examined him carefully. When he had finished, he gave a look which those about could interpret. Olive burst into tears. The Bishop, with a single fierce effort, took her hand in his, and pressed it gratefully. His lips moved again. No sound escaped them; but the words he framed were "Thank God," and Evelyn instantly read them.

Hour after hour passed away through that fatal Sunday. By seven at night, the Bishop rallied a little in a dying flicker. He held up one hand as if he wished to speak. Evelyn, who was nearest at the moment, bent over him.

The Bishop whispered in her ear. His voice, though thick, was distinctly audible. "The Lord has been good to me," he said. "He has spared me that last humiliation, and your mother that sorrow. Let him punish me now as he will! I shall never speak again. I am coming into port. Good bye, dear, and kiss me!"

She kissed him passionately. So did Olive. Then he fell back and said no more. Five minutes later, the heavy breathing ceased. Olive hid her face in her hands. Evelyn stooped again and kissed the lips of a man who, whatever his sin, had died heroically.

Sir Nathaniel drew Yate-Westbury aside into the passage. "Under these circumstances," he said, "it is unnecessary for anybody to inquire whether the story which you and I alone know, and that very partially, was true or a delusion."

"Oh, certainly," Yate-Westbury answered. "I shall tell Mrs. Glisson and her daughter that he died from nervous strain, resulting in paralysis; and that the strain was due to his excessive anxiety about the affairs of his diocese."

Evelyn came out to them, in tears. "Mother need never know," she said, "what troubled him in his last few days."

"*Nobody* will ever know," Yate-Westbury answered, lying like a gentleman and a Christian. "There was nothing in it. I am convinced it was all premonition of this paralysis, acting upon an abnormally excited brain. He had been worrying over this question of the pretended orders; and it killed a frame already weary with much toil for others. Your father was a good man. We could more easily have spared half a dozen stock bishops."

"Then you don'' believe it was true?" Evelyn cried, herself half doubting.

The specialist perjured himself like a man. "Not one word of it!" he answered.

Evelyn broke down utterly. "Oh thank you," she cried. "Thank you! I *am* so glad for Mother. Though myself, I should have loved him just the same, no matter what he had done. He was my father, Sir Nathaniel, and the best and sweetest father any girl ever had. I should have believed in him if he had committed a dozen murders. I should have known they were right —because he did them!"

THE END.